# THE SHADOW SOCIETY

## SHADOW GUARDIANS ACADEMY

*USA TODAY* BESTSELLING AUTHOR
# ELLE SCOTT

Edited by: Janet Minchin Hanna
Cover design: Moorbooks Design

www.ellescottbooks.com

ISBN: 978-0-6488125-0-0

# BOOKS BY ELLE SCOTT

## THE INCANDESCENT SERIES
Ray of Light
Harbour of Light
Symphony of Light

## SHADOW GUARDIANS
Ever Marked
Ever Fallen
... plus more to come

## SHADOW GUARDIANS ACADEMY
The Shadow Society
... plus more to come

## BEHIND GLASS SERIES
Behind Glass
... plus more to come

## BE A PART OF THE TEAM
www.facebook.com/groups/ellescottstreetteam

The easiest choices are the ones we feel intuitively

# ONE

Hiding fangs or talons or sometimes wings was no easy feat.

*Rule One: It is forbidden to show your true self to civilians.*
*Rule Two: Protect not kill.*
*Rule Three: Be careful who you trust.*

Seventeen-year-old Sage Windsor replayed the rules in her mind on a loop as if her whole life depended on it. Since the moment she'd woken up that morning, a sinking feeling haunted her. The feeling remained through breakfast, through first period, through lunch. It stuck like glue, spreading from the pit of her stomach and forming as a lump in her throat. As though she knew something big was about to happen. Not bad or good, just something.

Sage stared at her feet as she scurried down the corridor at Graystone Boarding Academy. Her best friend Camila strutted beside her, shoulders rolled back with pride. Camila's confident gaze fell on each fellow student she passed as if daring them to look at her. In contrast, when anyone happened to glance their way, Sage would avert her eyes and let her purple hair fall in a frame around her face.

"What's wrong with you today?" Camila side-eyed Sage, looking up and down her body.

Stopping at her locker, Sage peered through the strands of her hair and shrugged. "I don't know. I've just got a funny feeling."

"Is it that time of the month?"

"What? No." Sage flung the back of her hand against Camila's bicep. "It's more instinctual, like my body is warning me."

Camila stopped and clapped her hands together. With wide kohl eyes she leaned in close and whispered, "Animalistic instincts?"

"Shhh," Sage hushed, checking over her shoulder.

She felt like all eyes were on her, watching her every move, judging and waiting for her to reveal her true self. But they were all too wrapped up in their own selves to notice.

"Don't shoosh me," Camila said, wagging a finger. "I'm only trying to understand which part of you is off kilter."

Sage didn't even know. It was hard enough to understand how she could do the things she could, let alone understand some airy-fairy emotion. Sighing, she opened her locker and pulled out a workbook. The pages inside the book were empty bar a few random doodles. She technically didn't need it for her next class, but she clutched it to her chest with meaning anyway. She didn't need the book because her next "class" wasn't technically on the curriculum. The book was all for show. A misleading lie. Those were the lengths someone went to when they were carrying a secret.

"Um, Sage?" A soft unknown voice said from behind.

*Here we go,* Sage thought. Two words from a stranger was all it took to convince her what the unwelcome feeling was about. She'd flown under the radar all semester and finally someone was going to say something.

Sage turned to face the girl. She looked like a sophomore, tall yet not quite grown into her body. Smiling nervously, she said, "You probably don't remember me. I'm Harriot, I was one of the freshmen who helped you out with your philanthropy project last year? Anyway, I really like your hair. Can I ask what brand you used to dye it? I've been wanting to go red or orange for ages, but I'm worried it will fade too quickly."

"Harriot?" Sage repeated, thinking back to not even six months ago. A flicker of a memory surfaced. "You grew over Summer."

The bell signaled the start of the next period. Ignoring it, Harriot smiled fully and opened her mouth to speak. But before any words came out, Camila stepped between them.

Camila bared her teeth and jutted her chin, hissing like a stray cat. She remained that way, like some kind of relapsed sociopath, until Harriot backed away. Once satisfied with the space between them, Camila let her bottom lip roll out.

Still watching Harriot, she leaned toward Sage. "It's best we keep our distance from civilians. Isn't that what Makoto says?"

"Makoto says to be careful, not rude," Sage said with a light-hearted tone.

"I *was* being careful. Her next question was going to be about the *you know what*." Camila whispered the last part as if saying the words "Shadow Society" aloud would bring unwanted attention.

She was probably right, and Sage knew it. They'd dodged questions before, but it was much better to be hurtful than even giving a sliver of truth away. Especially for Sage, whose emotions always seemed to reveal themselves involuntarily. Like somehow she'd give herself away from the simple twitch of an eye and they'd see right through her act. She was not so great at shrugging off attention... not like Camila.

The Shadow Society was well known at the Academy and according to the whispers across campus, it was just a fancy name for a group of honor kids with ultra-rich parents who bought their way in. Sage hoped that was the case, anyway, because looking a little closer, there was no denying something weird was going on. As soon as both of them had joined the society, their appearances changed. Softer hair, more defined features, muscles that seemed to grow overnight.

Sage ran her hand through her silken hair, once a tangle of frizz, and closed her locker. Sage watched Harriot walk past with her friends, whispering and scowling in Camila's direction. The swirling inside her stomach kept churning like it had all day. But now it was mixed with guilt.

"It's better to let them take their guesses," Camila continued. "They'll never know the truth."

That was the worst part of being a part of the society. Even after a full semester, Sage still hadn't gotten use to pushing people away for their own safety. She shook off the uneasy feeling and nodded.

Camila slid her arm through Sage's and together they walked through the emptying corridor. Tugging Sage in close, Camila said, "We'll always have each other."

Sage let her smile grow. Camila always knew how to make her feel better. Meeting her in the Shadow Society was her saving grace. She'd finally found somewhere she belonged.

As they swung a left and ascended the stairs a rush of footsteps thumped behind them. Within a few moments, a flash of platinum blonde hair appeared beside them and Nadya, another society member, glared her sky-blue eyes in their direction. Still jogging, she said, "Do you like being late?"

"I like to live on the edge," Camila stated.

Nadya frowned and puffed ahead. Sage swung her

head to Camila and in synchrony they rolled their eyes. Sage liked to give everyone the benefit of the doubt, but Nadya made it so hard.

They followed her as she swung open a door and slid inside the room where their secrets were kept. Hiding behind locked doors, boarded windows, and sound-proof padding lived the truth of who those recruits really were... what they had become.

They were Shape-shifters. Or, more specifically, Shadow Guardians. And their purpose was to protect the innocent and work in secret.

# TWO

For Sage, being chosen felt like a lifetime ago. She'd just won the prestigious humanitarian award for her volunteer work at the orphanage and next minute she was invited by Makoto to join the mysterious group. And now, she was one of five exclusive butts sitting inside a large theater-style lecture room.

"It takes a certain type of person to become a True Guardian."

She'd heard her mentor, Makoto, say that line countless times. About how lucky they were. How special they must be to be one of only five students chosen. He was selective, only choosing the best of the best.

But that particular day his words didn't feel as empowering as he meant them to be. All it really did was instill a panic in Sage that fed the already growing knot in her stomach. She began to wonder if maybe he'd made a mistake and somehow she would stuff it all up.

Makoto looked to be of Japanese descent and was strikingly handsome with styled black hair and a strong jawline. He also looked like he was barely hitting thirty years old, but his true age was over a thousand. At least, that's what Sage liked to think.

He'd never told them his age but had mentioned he was one of the first Guardians ever, so she'd assumed he was ancient.

An elbow dug into Sage's ribs, followed by a whispered, "Blah blah blah, when are we going to get to the juicy stuff?"

She glanced sideways. Camila gave a sly smile then exaggerated a yawn. As she brought her hand away from her mouth, she flicked her wavy brown ponytail over her tanned shoulders and winked.

"Shhh..." Sage hushed, trying not to laugh.

Three sets of eyes flicked to the two girls as they sat at the back of room. Sage would often mentally defend herself by thinking that they didn't sit at the back, back. But technically, even if they were on the fourth last row, there was no one else behind them. She fained a smile and slumped deep into her seat.

This year's recruits weren't exactly inseparable yet, not like previous years. After she'd found a closeness with Camila, she was waiting for the moment where the rest of them clicked and became a solid team. She wished they'd at least try to make an effort, but if she was honest with herself, she and Camila didn't exactly make it easy for them. Regardless, she cared for them anyway. They were practically all she had.

"Now, you know that when you half-shift and you align with your Guardian, you gain certain attributes." Makoto paced in front of his desk, gliding his finger along the timber as he moved. At the edge of his unbuttoned collar a dark shape on his skin peeked through. It was a spiral, a black tattoo-like marking.

Sage had one too. They all did. It was the mark of a Guardian—the gateway to the Veil and the door in which their Guardian animal stepped through.

Makoto continued, "For carnivores, we grow fangs and claws mostly. But for others, it's a little more random. Can anyone tell me why this is?"

A hand in the front row shot up. Sage stared at the straight arm reaching for the sky. It belonged to

Nadya. Top of the class Nadya. Camila moaned.

Nadya was the perfect example of a True Guardian. It was worse that she knew it, too. Which often made Sage wonder if she herself wouldn't make a good Guardian, because she sure as hell didn't want to be like Nadya.

"Well, those attributes need to grow from human parts. And if there are no human parts similar to the Guardian's, then it gets a little complicated. The Guardian randomly chooses which attributes to grow." Even staring at the back Nadya's head, Sage could imagine the arrogant pout on her face.

"Right." Makoto lifted his finger off his desk and pointed to Nadya. His finger followed the seats above her until it rested on Sage. "Can you tell the class what it feels like to have your attribute grow?"

Sage felt heat rush to her cheeks. Ugh. She hated when he called her out in class. Especially when it was to talk about her specific Guardian.

A barn owl. A freaking barn owl. When she first became a Guardian at the start of the school year, she'd secretly been a little disappointed that an owl chose her to be its human counterpart. Especially when Camila got to have a cool animal like a cougar.

When she wasn't shifted, the owl sat beside her, hidden in the Veil and unseen by human eyes. Its feathers were a mix of white and fawny tan and she could sense its beady eyes staring up at her. Watching. Waiting for her to call it forward. It was small and unassuming, yes, but also fierce. After Makoto taught her how to fly, she'd grown to like it.

She had to like it. After all, they were connected with a special bond that would last a lifetime.

But still, whenever she spoke about it a sense of embarrassment lingered, as though she was being judged.

Sage tucked a finger underneath the black, leather choker that firmly hugged her neck. It belonged to her late-mother, and she'd worn it every day for the last ten years. "It's, uhh, fine. I don't know. It just feels like someone is poking my back and then they're there."

She was talking about the wings. Yes, while everyone else grew fangs and claws, she got wings and talons. Nothing really to complain about, except they weren't that easy to hide.

Makoto smiled and nodded in thanks. His eyes twitched and the irises that once were brown turned flaming gold. As his smile grew, so did his canines, reaching over his bottom lips. At the tips of his fingers, long claws replaced his nails.

"Now," he said. "Watch the shift."

To Sage's eyes, Makoto looked like a human in desperate need of a manicure and a dentist appointment. She called her owl to her, and when they were aligned, she could see so much more. The world a human couldn't see.

Between the normal world and the Veil, a wolf appeared. It stood in line with Makoto like a ghost and its golden aura encased them both. They were one. Aligned.

That was the half-shift.

Makoto said, "Watch carefully."

There was a flicker in the connection and Makoto's wolf stepped forward. It looked the same to Sage, except the wolf was in front. To a human eye, though...

Sage returned to human form, letting her owl move back beside her. Makoto's human body was nowhere to be seen. In his place, was his wolf; large, with thick, jet-black fur. Real enough to touch.

The full shift.

The wolf howled; nose aimed in Sage's direction. Another elbow to her rib. She whipped her head to Camila and two bronze eyes stared back. Through her fangs, Camila hissed, "He wants you to see the next bit properly."

Sage called her owl back so she could see the Guardian and Makoto in their true form. When

Makoto seemed satisfied that she was ready, he pointed at his wolf. "Watch."

In an instant, his wolf moved back to his side taking not even half a second to shift.

"How the hell?" Down the front, next to Nadya, Caspar leaned forward. His Guardian's blue eyes stared in the space where Makoto's wolf had been. "You didn't half-shift to return?"

Caspar was a bit of an enigma. Sage never knew where his allegiance sat. He was Nadya's sidekick, but there was a kindness to his eyes that drew her in. Not a speck of hair was out of place on his buzz cut, and his dark-brown, dreamy eyes matched his unblemished skin. And that jawline, it was something to behold—the moment Sage met him she thought he'd be the perfect male model.

"It's about control. Knowing your Guardian, working together as a team. You could miss the half-shift phase all together if you want. Although, it is my favorite phase. Our *strongest* phase."

"Mine, too," Nadya said and Sage wondered if she was just saying that to appease Makoto.

"That. Was. Epic!" a voice cried from the side.

Arielle sat by herself on the edge of the lecture room. Her natural red hair bobbed on her shoulders as she clapped with excitement. Aligned with her Guardian—a ginger house cat—her neon green eyes flashed around the room, beaming at her classmates.

Everyone seemed surprised and Sage frowned as she looked at all their faces. *Wasn't shifting like that normal?* She wondered. She'd been doing that from the beginning. Sometimes growing bulky, not-so-subtle wings between the shifts was the last thing she wanted.

Makoto stared at Arielle, brows dropping as though wondering if she was being sarcastic or not. He must have decided that she was because he cleared his throat and walked back to his desk, sitting on the chair behind it.

With only a few minutes left of class, Sage sighed and pulled a pencil from behind her ear. She pressed the lead onto paper and began to draw. Her long dyed-purple hair fell onto the paper, it's lighter ends covering the spiral she darkened, around and around. She'd dyed her hair to match her owl, who had a bright purple aura. When she was half-shifted, her eyes shone like violet dipped in glow-in-the-dark paint.

"I've got a new assignment for you all," Makoto said.

"Separate ones?" Camila enthused.

Makoto chortled. "One day, Camila, one day. But this one is a team assignment. I'll give the lead to..."

Sage looked up from her drawing and shared a bored glance with Camila. They both whispered, "Nadya."

"Arielle."

"Whaaaaaa?" Arielle cried, jumping out of her seat. "Me? Really? Oh, my goodness, sir. I won't let you down."

"Oh God," Camila moaned.

"It could be worse," Sage said, closing her notepad.

"The assignment starts now. You're to meet in the library immediately, you'll know your mission when you see it." Makoto glanced to the clock at the exact same moment the bell rang out.

Anticipating his next words, no one moved an inch.

"Repeat the rules."

In unison, the five recruits recited the same thing they did at the end of every class.

"I work in secret and won't show my true self to civilians. I protect the innocent and won't kill unless they are a Fallen. I am careful with who I trust so I won't turn anyone until I graduate."

Sage had no idea she'd break two of those rules by night fall.

# THREE

The five of them walked across campus together. Nadya and Caspar in front, Sage and Camila behind, and Arielle bounced around in between. Graystone Academy's buildings were old and, contrary to its name, made of sandstone, except for the dorms, which sat on the hill that overlooked the campus. The dorms were modern with rendered exterior painted in pale yellow—like they were made to fit but kind of didn't. In between the clashing of worlds was the football field. And a forest—dense and evergreen—surrounded them all.

The pathways around the three main academy buildings were made of cobblestone and Sage winced as she watched Arielle skip along, gracefully avoiding the unleveled ground. Sage was waiting for Arielle to trip, but she never did. It shouldn't have surprised her. When she was turned by Makoto, Sage learned that the best part about becoming a Shadow Guardian wasn't necessarily the shifting ability. It was the growth in muscle, stamina, intelligence, agility.

"The boys are out!" Camila drawled. Her eyes were fixed on the football team running onto the field for practice.

The academy was well known for their stellar

varsity team. Unbeaten in three years, they were the heroes of the school. Which was good for The Shadow Society, taking unwanted eyes away.

Sage raised an eyebrow and teased, "Even after being turned, you're still drawn to brainless dimwits?"

"Hey!" Caspar said, looking over his shoulder. His striking eyes pierced through her. "Not all are brainless."

Another thing that Sage shouldn't have been surprised by. Guardians senses were heightened, too. Better sight, taste, sound.

Caspar leered at her from a good ten feet away. His brother, Owen, was smart. Really smart. He'd gotten a scholarship on his grades alone. And, he was a part of the varsity team she'd just insulted.

Sage grinned apologetically. "Sorry."

"Mhmm," Camila whispered, waving her hand at Caspar. "And his brother is fi-ine. He can rub his chocolate-skinned body over mine any day."

"Heard that," Caspar said as they stopped outside the library.

They pressed their noses to the window, five eager faces scanning the two storey building. A new assignment was always exciting. Who needed protecting? How would they get to use their abilities to do it?

Looking inside the library, two floors of books circled the walls. At the back of the room, a few single cubicles hid in corners behind a grand piano. Sage had always wondered what a piano was doing in a library, but figured it was more for show than practical use. In the middle, larger tables were scattered around for group study. On one of the tables, a freshman hunched over a book, he pushed his glasses up and nervously looked around as though expecting something.

"That kid looks weak," Camila stated. "He's gotta be our assignment."

"Not all people who look weak, are weak," Nadya

clapped back.

"His name is AJ," Caspar said. "He's president of the chess club."

Camila turned her back and leaned against the window frame. She picked at her fingers and sighed. "Of course he is."

Sage watched as another boy walked across the library. He was tall and toned and even from where she was, she could tell he was gorgeous. The boy grabbed a chair from beside AJ and spun it around. He straddled the chair, resting his elbows over the back.

"And that's Mason," Caspar explained, staring through the glass. "He's a bit of a loner and always seems to have an arrogant grin planted on his face."

Camila pushed herself off the window and turned around. "Do you know everybody?"

The edges of Caspar's lips lifted into a proud kind of smile. "Yep."

"Shoosh," Nadya hissed. She strained her neck as though the minute movement would help her hear better.

Mason scrunched up the sleeves of his unbuttoned blazer, showcasing bandages around both his wrists. His knuckles were covered in scratches and bruises. AJ grimaced as Mason leaned forward, tapping aggressively on the study book. He raised his hands, shaking his head in submission.

Caspar guffawed. "Man, I hate it when people think they're God's gift. Mason's dad was some middle-weight boxing champion, so it doesn't surprise me his son would be an entitled jerk."

Sage muffled a laugh. Caspar darted his eyes her way and his head soon followed. As he gave her a questioning glare, she shrugged and with a soft voice she said, "You're just sounding a bit jealous."

"Well... I'm not," Caspar spluttered, turning away from the eyes that were now on him.

"Sorry Cass." Nadya placed her hand on his

shoulder. "But I agree with Sage. We need to be level-headed, we can't let our insecurities drive our decisions."

"Ugh," Camila groaned. "Is this seriously our assignment? To save a dweeb from a bully? I could do that without being a Guardian, you know?"

"We get what we're given." Nadya sighed and turned to Arielle. "What're your orders, boss?"

The question seemed to spark Arielle to life. Her eyes widened, looking around the group in excitement. She'd been standing there, silent and unassuming, as if waiting for the invitation to begin her task as leader.

Bouncing on her heels, Arielle bit her lip. After a few rushed breaths, she said, "Okay. You're right, Cami. We probably don't even need our Guardians for it. Remember what Makoto says about only bringing them when needed? Nadya and Caspar, you guys, take the high ground. In case this rough-head escapes to the mezzanine. Camila, you and I will intervene, no shifting, just talk. And, Sage, your little owl could make a great distraction."

Sage felt her whole body become heavy. She was always the distraction. As if an owl couldn't do anything else.

As they walked towards the entrance, Camila muttered, "This is so boring. I want something with substance."

Nadya held the door open, and with a cavalier smile, she said, "One step at a time."

Camila faced Sage, rolling her eyes as they walked in, and everyone spread out into their respective locations.

Sage made a bee-line for an empty cubicle down the back. As she hurried past the large tables, she glanced at their assignment.

AJ's eyes were lowered as his bully stood above him. Mason ripped through a study book, tearing out page after page and sprinkling them over AJ's head like rain. Sage felt her stomach tighten. Seeing someone innocent being treated as if they didn't matter went against everything she stood for.

She was almost ready to abandon Arielle's plan and head right to Mason herself. But then he looked up, wild eyes falling on her. He stared at her for a second, face relaxing as he watched her scurry to the cubicle. By the time she sat down, he'd returned his attention to AJ.

She cowered out of sight behind the petition, ready to act fast. Calling her owl forward, she let it pass right through into full shift. Without waiting another moment, she took flight. Sage didn't want to head straight for Mason, that would be a mistake. She could cause him to act out of fear and nothing good ever came from that.

So instead, she flew in a direct line for the piano. Her tiny feet landed on the keys and a gentle sound filled the air. She pranced her talons across the ivories, little legs sending an awkward tune of chopsticks into the high-roofed room. It would have been humiliating—making her owl dance on a grand piano for a diversion—but she couldn't help but smile. What a sight it must have been.

Mason glanced across to the unusual commotion. His eyebrows shot up, shocked and confused. That was all they needed: Camila and Arielle pounced, pulling Mason away from AJ. His gaze switched between the two of them as they dragged him across the library. Almost as if resigning to the fact he'd been overthrown, he slumped his shoulders and let them take him without a fight. He settled his eyes back on Sage's owl and stared at her, bewildered and defeated. His gaze remained until Camila pushed him outside and slammed the doors in his face.

The way he looked through the entrance of the library gave Sage pause. He seemed lost. Disheartened.

The knot in her gut twisted around itself. She quickly flew back to the cubicle and hid behind the dividers. Peering up to the mezzanine, Sage saw

Caspar and Nadya run for the stairs. Aligned with her Guardian she could see theirs beside them, a wolf and fox respectively. Both their auras shone bright neon blue as they swiftly found their way to AJ, making sure he was all right. Camila and Arielle sauntered over next, the four of them hovering over AJ like he was a little lost puppy.

But Sage couldn't have cared less about AJ in that moment. Every breath she took, the knot inside her grew. She shifted back into her human form and slowly stood, her eyes boring through the window.

Outside the library windows, Mason paced up and down the cobblestone path, muttering to himself. Swiveling at the edge of the building, he raked his hands through his hair and lifted his gaze. His deep-green irises landed on her.

As their eyes locked, the storm that had brewed in the pit of her stomach all day suddenly ceased.

And then she knew. They had it wrong. AJ wasn't the assignment. Mason was.

# FOUR

After lunch and some fair fussing over AJ later, Sage sat through her math class thinking of one thing only. Mason.

Surely, he wasn't the assignment. Surely a cocksure, loner-on-purpose, chisel-jawed, jerk-wad wasn't the assignment. But she couldn't get him out of her head.

She knew that hurting people hurt people. Maybe he was in pain. Maybe his heart was so broken he didn't know how to fix it. Maybe he had a horrible upbringing?

She stiffened. Well, with the death of both her parents and begrudgingly taken in by an uncaring aunt, she had a pretty awful childhood—but that didn't cause her to take it out on others. In fact, it made her want to be better to people because you never know what someone is going through.

Ugh, and there it was. She had no idea what he was going through. Dammit. Sage had to find out. The constant ache in her stomach begged her to.

As soon as the bell rang, Sage bustled out of class and headed straight for her locker. Throwing her books inside, she began to consider where she might find Mason.

"I didn't mean to," a fearful squeak came from down the hall.

Sage peered around her locker door. Halfway down the corridor, Mason had bailed up a freshman. He scuffed the poor soul's collar and held him up against the wall.

*Well, that was easy,* Sage thought.

"Don't give me that garbage," Mason scowled, clutching the boys collar in his fists. He gave a quick side-eye to Sage, then returned to the boy. "I saw you do it."

"W... What are you talking about? Maybe... maybe it was someone else who looked... who looked like me," the boy stammered.

Mason clenched his jaw and pulled the boy closer to him. Again, he glanced at Sage almost as if he was reveling in the attention she gave. Turning back to the boy, he used full force and slammed the flailing body against the wall. "You little weasel. It was you. I won't let you go till you admit it."

Sage's Guardian instincts switched into high alert. She quickly glanced over her shoulder to make sure no one was looking and shifted. Her insides swirled with adrenalin as she flew with speed towards the altercation. Even if Mason was the assignment, even if there was something more to him than being one big bully, she couldn't let him hurt the boy like that.

As she approached, she began flapping her wings against lockers. Clack, clack, clack. Mason swiveled and when his eyes rested on the owl, he dropped the boy. Mouth agape, he stared; and the boy ran off.

Satisfied, Sage turned and flew back from where she came. Safe behind the full-length locker she shifted into human form. As soon as she did, fingers ripped the edge of her locker.

Sage watched in horror as Mason opened the door wider than it should go. Hinges cracked as he looked beyond her into the corridor. "Did you see that?"

With her heart in her throat, she replied with the only angle she could. A lie. "See what?"

Mason frowned, bringing his attention to her. He glanced her up and down. "You're Sage, right?"

"How do you—" Sage began.

"I asked people," he interrupted. Nodding at her head, he explained, "Bright purple hair is the giveaway."

"Right." Sage felt her eyebrows drop. She turned to look inside her locker. Having a conversation wasn't part of the plan. She wanted to follow him to his dorm room and see what his deal was. Not get to know him on a personal level. If she wanted to do that, she'd tell him what a dick he'd been to those boys today.

"You were in the library today." He stated, still holding onto her locker. "Did you see the owl in there, playing the piano?"

Sage felt her throat dry up. She was used to hiding what she was, but the direct question threw her off. Shuffling papers inside her locker, she kept up with the lie and mumbled, "Owl?"

Mason huffed and snapped his hand away from her locker. Sage had to catch the door before it swung in her face. Without saying goodbye, Mason rushed off. Sage closed her locker, watching him storm towards the entrance, shaking his head.

"Oh my goodness, are you okay?" a sweet voice said from behind her. Sage spun on her heels to see Arielle approach with Camila close behind her.

"He's charming," Camila said, thick with sarcasm.

"Mm," Sage glanced over her shoulder and watched Mason head towards the dorms. Her stomach wound into a knot—something she didn't want to get used to. The reason for it eluded her. The only thing she knew was that she *had* to go after him. Turning back, she said, "Do you think I should follow him to make sure he doesn't bully anyone on his way to the dorms?"

Camila nodded. "That's probably a really great

idea, I'll come with you."

"Well, hold on," Arielle said with her hands on her hips. "Ain't I the boss of this assignment?" She pouted, then erupted in giggles as if the whole thing was a joke.

"Well," Sage said, trying not to sound exasperated. "What do you say we do about him, boss?

Arielle pinched her chin between two fingers, her eyes thoughtfully dancing between Camila and Sage. She whipped her hand away and decisively said, "Okay! Camila and I will check on AJ, while you follow him. Is that all right?"

Sage nodded and Arielle's freckled nose scrunched in delight. She threaded her arm through Camila's and tugged at her to follow. Camila gave Sage a half-grimace, half-smile, and Sage could tell that Arielle was growing on her.

"I'm coming, geez!" Camila teased, slipping her arm from Arielle's hold. She stepped closer to Sage and said, "Be careful, would you? I have a weird feeling about him. Tell me everything."

The knot in Sage's stomach subsided the moment she caught sight of Mason again. He was on the other side of the field, turning up the path for the boys' dorm. She ran to catch up. As she charged up the hill, she noticed him walk directly past the entrance and straight for the parking lot.

She watched as Mason jumped on a motorbike and started the engine. Just her luck. This wasn't going to be easy after all.

Sage took a deep breath and resigned to the fact that this assignment was going to test her limits. And as Mason revved his bike and sped off down the driveway, she ran into the surrounding forest and called her owl forward.

# FIVE

Graystone Academy was location on part of a thirty acre property. It was surrounded by the forest that cornered Ever Valley National Park. The closest town, Burrville, was a ten mile drive through a winding forest road to the base of the foothills.

Sage took flight through the trees, knowing it would take Mason at least five minutes to get to the main road. If she was quick enough, she could take a short-cut through the forest and be able to follow him from there. As she reached the main road, she took rest on a high branch and closed her eyes. Sure enough, there was the low hum of a bike, rumbling towards the road.

When Mason sped past, she flew behind him, sticking to the treetops and hoping he wouldn't see her. Even though his bike was twenty times louder, she still cringed every time her wings whipped through the cool air. As if the slight noise will give her away.

On the outskirts of Burrville, Mason swung a right at the old brewery and continued along a gravel road. Not far along, the road narrowed and ended at a parking lot. Three buildings were set off the end of the road. A pottery workshop, a mechanic, and a boxing studio in between them. They all looked the same—old and run down with weeds growing from their bases and rust lining their roofs. Sage stopped and found a tree to curl her talons around.

Mason slowed his bike and parked at the opening of an alley alongside the studio. He entered the building below the flicker of a neon light that spelled "bo - ing club". Sage stayed in the shadows, using her owl's vision to spy through the small, steel barred window out the front. She could see Mason greeting a man in his mid-twenties with a quick shoulder tap.

"Hey bro," he said, as some kind of hello.

*Well, that's that,* she thought to herself, wondering if she'd made a mistake in the heat of the moment. Maybe he wasn't the assignment after all. Maybe he simply was just a jerk with a chip on his shoulder.

Watching as he hung his blazer over a fold-out chair and unbutton his shirt, Sage decided he definitely didn't need her help. He was toned. Muscles curving in all the right places, divots and lines that formed a six pack. No, he didn't need her help at all.

As he tugged his bandages over his knuckles his eyes flicked to the window. Even though there was no way he could have seen her up the tree from that distance, she backed along the branch, just in case. She watched him as he stepped into the ring and bounced from foot to foot.

Satisfied that she was wrong, Sage sighed and turned back toward campus. But she only made it half a mile before a small knot pinged in her stomach. She didn't know why, and she couldn't have explained it to anyone, it was just a feeling—she *had* to go back.

The tips of her wings grazed pine nettles as she swept around. *Quicker,* her instincts urged her. Silently, she scolded herself for leaving him alone. The heavy feeling of dread sunk her heart to her feet and back.

She burst through the tree line and flew right across the parking lot, swooping over Mason's bike and stopping just short of the window.

Hovering, breathless, she peered in.

Mason was still in the ring, a slight grimace on his face as he stared at his opponent. Another boy with similar height and weight jumped with light feet around him. Four men in suits sat in a line outside of the ropes. The man Mason greeted earlier stood beside them—his teeth sunk into a red apple as his eyes bore into Mason's back.

The opponent threw a right hook that landed square on Mason's right shoulder. The force sent Mason backward at the same time the man with the apple yelled, "hands up".

Mason raised his hands, but it was too late, a left jab slammed against his cheek. Mason fell to the ropes, clutching them to stop from falling. As he took a moment to catch his breath, blood pooled at the corner of his mouth.

Sage urged forward, her talons circling the steel bars in front of the window. As quick as the flash of empathy appeared, she pushed it away, ashamed to be cheering for a bully. Confusion soon followed. What was the knot in her stomach? Surely, it wasn't to stop him from fighting in a normal boxing match?

The man outside the ring ran to Mason, veins popping on his forehead. He spat bits of half-chewed apple flesh as he hissed, "Get up, boy."

Mason stared at him for a moment before giving a quick nod. He wiped his mouth and pushed off the ropes to face his opponent. Sage held her breath as Mason dodged a swinging arm, slamming his fist into his opponent's ribs.

*Yes!* She cheered to herself, throwing her wings up in celebration. But she'd gotten so excited she'd forgotten where she was, what she was. Her wings flapped against the window pane as she lowered them.

She froze as Mason's eyes darted for a split second meeting her neon purples'. That split second was long enough. He squeezed his eyes in a long blink and ...

*Thwack!* Another blow to his jaw.

Mason's eyes rolled to the ceiling and he fell, chest hitting the ground.

For what felt like forever, Sage sat in her human form on the roof of the pottery workshop, which shared an alley with the boxing studio. She'd seen the men in suits leave with the opponent almost immediately after the fight but after another thirty minutes there was still no sign of Mason. He'd been knocked out and her stomach was in turmoil just thinking about it.

She cussed to herself about what a terrible Guardian she made. One that only got put in charge of distractions—she'd become so good at that she did it unintentionally, too. She felt awful that he'd lost because of her... that he was hurt because of her. So, as the sun inched for the horizon, there she was, waiting for a bully to see if he was okay. But it could have been more than that too, if he was in fact the assignment.

The side door of the studio opened into the alley and Sage leaned forward. Mason stepped out, back in his school uniform, with white strips across his eyebrow and dried blood along his bottom lip. A bandage wound around one of his wrists, halfway to his elbow. It looked newly dressed and for a second Sage wondered when he'd hurt himself there during the fight, but then she remembered he'd had it on in the library earlier.

"Mason?" A gruff voice boomed from within the studio.

A grimace made its way across Mason's face. He quickly closed the door and rushed down the alley toward his bike. Sage tried not to breathe as he passed right below her.

"Mason?" The voice cried again. The door swung open with such a force it slammed into a dumpster behind it. "Did I say you could leave?"

"I've got school tomorrow, Ben. Can't it wait?"

The way the man tightened his jaw gave Sage chills. She leaned further forward and half-shifted, letting her talons dig into the roof for support. Two giant wings reached from her shoulder blades. She didn't know what for, but she was ready.

"Can what wait?" Ben growled.

Mason's shoulders slumped. Still facing the parking lot at the end of the alley, he said, "The impending lecture. I'm just.... Tired."

"You're tired?" Ben scoffed. Even the way his boots hit the gravel felt threatening. "How selfish do you want to be? Do you know how embarrassing that was? To have my own brother lose so pathetically in pre-selection. We have to wait a whole three months for the next tournament."

Wait? Brother? Sage didn't know whether to feel relieved or even more alarmed.

She stared at Mason as he stopped at his bike, a gentle hand smoothing over his helmet. "I'm sorry."

That wasn't the Mason she'd seen earlier. That wasn't the confident cocky jerk who thought he was too good for the world. No, that boy, right there, he was broken.

"What?" Ben teased with indignation. "I can't hear you?"

Mason's fists tightened and his jaw clenched as he spun. "I'm sorry, okay? Is that what you want? I'm sorry that I can't follow in dad's mighty footsteps. I'm sorry that you aren't strong enough to do it yourself."

The moment Mason stopped talking, he winced as though he knew he shouldn't have said those words. Ben lurched forward and without warning, slammed his fist into Mason's already bruised eye. Mason fell back onto his bike, causing it to crash with him to the ground.

A hint of anger bubbled in Sage's chest. She watched in horror as Ben stood over Mason's weakened body and landed a punch right into his abdomen. "You're a sniveling piece of shit, Mase. I can't believe we're the same blood. Dad pays your tuition at that fancy boarding school and this is the thanks he gets? You're lucky I don't call him and tell him what a disgrace you are to his name."

Wheezing, Mason glared up into his brother's spiteful eyes. "Ben, please—"

Sage leapt to her feet, her purple eyes blazing. Surely, Ben wouldn't aim to hurt his brother. Just a little roughening up, like siblings sometimes do. She waited for him to stop.

But he didn't. Ben slammed his knuckles against Mason's rib cage. Once, twice, three times.

As Ben continued to pummel into an already beaten Mason, Sage shifted fully into her owl. She wasn't waiting any longer, it had gone on long enough. Now, wasn't the time for distractions. It wasn't the time for her to wonder whether she made a good Guardian. In that moment. It wasn't about her. It was about Mason and his life.

Swooping into the alley, Sage brought her legs in front of her and aimed. Her talons spread wide as she landed on Ben's head. Whipping her legs, she scratched at his face until he stumbled away from Mason. Arms flailing and blood pouring in lines down his face, Ben ran inside. She chased him just to make sure.

Shifting back into human form she ran for Mason to see if he was okay.

With swollen eyes, he stared, and with a shaky breath, he asked, "Sage?"

# SIX

Sage fell to her knees, inspecting his wounds. Mason's head rested on the gravel, blood oozing from his mouth and coating the ground in dark red. He coughed, eyes closing.

"Mason?" Sage asked. "Are you okay?"

"I saw you," he wheezed, clutching at his ribs. "I saw your... eyes... You were at the... you were at..." Mason spluttered, turning his face to the side as he coughed up more blood. He gave a weak spit and rolled his head back around. "You were at the window."

Sage swallowed. He'd seen her shift. He knew she was an owl.

She'd broken one of Makoto's rules but in that moment as she looked at him, contracting in pain, it didn't matter.

She tugged at his arm that covered his torso and moved it to the side. Gently, she lifted his shirt and inspected. Deep red swelled around two of his ribs. They were definitely broken.

"Do you have a phone?" she asked, moving her gaze to his face.

But his eyes were closed, his breathing labored.

"Mason?" she said, more urgently, tapping on his face. "Mason? I need you to wake up."

A muffled moan reverberated in the back of his throat and his eyes flickered open. Each breath he took was weaker than the last. She rested her ear to his chest, and using her heightened hearing, she listened to his heartbeat. It was faint and erratic and even with no first aid training, she knew that wasn't a good sign.

Her mind was a mix of thoughts. She needed to call an ambulance, someone who knew what they were doing. Her eyes darted to the studio door, wondering if she should risk calling for Ben. Would he even care? Would he want to finish the job? She glanced at his bike, laying on the ground. There was no way she could get them on that thing, she'd kill them both.

The only thing she could do was carry him to the hospital herself. She'd never tested her strength like that before, but now wasn't the time to hesitate. She clutched at his shoulders and hauled him into a sitting position.

Mason howled in agony. And as she reached to lift him up, he grabbed her wrist. "St... stop."

Sage cast her eyes to his hand as it softly circled her. And right there, peeking out of his unraveled bandage was a spiral mark—dark and black. Sage grabbed his arm, holding the mark toward the light to inspect it.

"You're a Guardian?" she asked.

Mason groaned, letting his body fall back to the ground.

Sage half-shifted, using her owl's vision to get a better look. It was a Guardian's mark all right. Except, there was a bright glow underneath it, shining like a beacon. He hadn't been turned yet, he was in incubation. Which meant—

Her heart raced as she looked up behind Mason. A transparent tiger with a red aura prowled around the bike, its gaze firmly on the mark. It was waiting, as all

Guardians did, for the transition. So that they and their human counterpart could become one.

She thought it strange, though, that he didn't seem to know what a Guardian was. True Guardians always informed and asked before marking, as Makoto had done with her. Unless. *Shit!* He'd been marked by a Fallen.

Droplets of cool rain began falling around them. Sage huddled over Mason, letting her wings open fully like an umbrella to protect him from the wet. Her hands shook as she wrapped his arm back in the bandage to stop the beacon for other Guardians. She didn't want to risk enticing one, especially a Fallen.

As she tied the bandage up, she said "Okay, buddy. You're going to have to let me carry you—"

She stopped talking the moment her eyes landed on his unmoving chest. Sage pushed her fingers to his neck, checking for a pulse. A lone beat tickled her fingertips, so faint she could barely feel it.

He was out of time.

And she was out of choices.

Sage ripped the bandage off again. She was a True Guardian and even though it was against the rules to turn someone before graduation, there was no way in hell she'd let him die. To save him, he'd need the speedy healing and strength of a Guardian.

Recalling Makoto's lesson on transition: carnivores use teeth, birds use talons. Sage spread her fingers wide and placed them on the spiral mark. Then, with a dry throat and a hopeful heart, she dug her talons into his flesh.

# SEVEN

Sage paced the length of her small dorm room. She took a few steps, paused at the door, then spun on her heels. She took another few steps to the window, sighed, and turned around to repeat the process. Camila stood in the middle of the room, her eyes floating between Mason and Sage.

It was eight in the morning and Sage hadn't slept a wink. After she'd turned Mason, she managed to carry him the whole way back to campus. Luckily, the night was dark and cloudy, so the sight of a girl lugging an unconscious boy through the halls wasn't so obvious. She'd kept her tired eyes glued to Mason the whole night and had lost count of the amount of times she'd checked his pulse. It was steady and strong, the way it should be. He'd also healed already—dried blood the only remnant from the night before. It was around seven-thirty when she decided she couldn't handle it anymore and called Camila.

"I broke two of Makoto's rules last night," Sage said, her hands raking through her unbrushed purple locks.

Camila guffawed. "All you had to do was kill someone and you'd have hit the trifecta!"

Sage stopped in her tracks and gave Camila the

side eye. "Seriously, what am I going to do?"

After a long sigh, Camila kicked Mason's foot. "Keep him as a pet?"

Rolling her eyes, Sage glanced at the clock. "He'll wake up soon, right? I don't remember being out of it for so long."

"God, don't you remember?" Camila plonked herself on Sage's bed. "I slept for a whole day after Makoto turned me."

Sage nodded. But it wasn't much comfort. Mason had no idea what he was about to become, and it was all her fault. She hovered over him, checking his pulse once more.

"Do you want me to cover for you?" Camila asked.

Sage let her fingers linger at his jaw line. He looked quite peaceful and kind while he slept. No fury wrinkles were creasing his brow. She let herself roll back to sit on the floor. Still looking at Mason, she replied, "If you don't mind? I probably need to be here when he wakes."

A sly smile hit Camila. She looked between Sage and Mason. Shaking her head, she sighed. "Oh lord, you are in so much trouble, girl."

"Huh?" Sage frowned. "Do you think Makoto will kick me out of the society? Can Guardians be un-Guardianed?"

"Don't think so, but that's not what I meant." Camila stared at Sage as if waiting for her to understand. When Sage didn't follow, she clasped her hands together. "This is kind of exciting if you think about it."

Sage glared at Camila wondering how on earth she could be so flippant in her time of need. She stood and said, "Oh, I've thought about it... all night. It's decidedly not exciting."

"Aww come on," Camila waved her hand dismissively. "Think about it. We have a mysterious Guardian who marked this sucker. And you, the superstar you are, saved him by making him a True.

We get to do a real mission, none of this protect a computer geek stuff."

"And dangerous. We don't know who marked him." Sage added with a whispered tone, "It could be a Fallen."

A glint cast over Camila's eyes. "Yes. That's the best part."

"Ugh." Sage fell face first onto her bed, her legs dangling over the edge. She flipped her head to Camila. "That would be the worst part. Girl, what the hell am I going to do? I'm dying here."

Camila jumped her legs under her and knelt over Sage. She grabbed her elbow and dragged her up. With a hand on each of Sage's shoulders, she said, "It's going to be fine. Trust me. Just go with it. This is what we signed up for."

"Maybe." Sage glanced over at Mason, still laying on the floor. Camila's enthusiasm began to seep in, and a small smile crept its way to the surface. "I guess it's a little exciting."

"That's the spirit!" Camila released her hold on Sage and leapt off the bed.

Sage's smile immediately turned into frown. "What if Makoto finds out?"

Camila moved to Sage's mirror and ran her fingers through her high ponytail. Casually, she replied, "Keep it a secret then. I'm sure as hell not gonna tell anyone. Although," she threw her thumb over her shoulder. "You will need to keep this buffoon in check, just while he's learning the basics."

Sage nodded in agreeance. Certainly couldn't have him running wild with his new abilities. That would be one sure fire way to not only get kicked from the society but the whole school, too.

The bell rang through the dorm building and Camila swung around. "What do you want me to tell him?"

"I'm uhh... I don't know. Say I'm sick."

Camila raised her brows and glared at Sage as if

she was an idiot. "We don't get sick, remember? Oh, I could say your aunt called?"

A pang burst through Sage's chest. Her aunt never called. She hissed her reply, "Just don't say anything. Pretend you haven't seen me."

" 'Atta girl." Camila grinned. "You've got this. You're stronger than you think. He will be a breeze."

# EIGHT

Sage stared at her alarm clock, watching the minutes tick over. It was past ten in the morning and Mason hadn't even flinched. She ran her finger between her neck and the leather necklace around it. Her knees, bent and cross-legged, bounced nervously on her bed.

She'd played a million different scenarios through her mind of Mason waking and her telling him the truth. Her imagination always took her to the darkest places. In one scenario, she blurted it immediately and he freaked out. She imagined him leaping out her unopened window, running across the campus with dried blood over his day-old uniform, and screaming about the underworld. In another scenario, she gave it to him in dribs and drabs, working her way to the fact he was now a shifter. He thought she was playing an elaborate prank.

Dropping her hands to her lap, she kneaded her knuckles and hoped that in the moment she'd find the right words. But how could she tell someone that they had become something without their choice? Something that would change their life forever.

A hand clutched the end of Sage's bed frame, followed by a loud gasp. Mason leapt to his feet, his disheveled hair falling over his startled green eyes. He spun in a full circle, stopping to face Sage. "How did I get here?"

Sage knelt up. Cautiously, she asked, "What do you remember?"

His eyes darted from her, to the bed, then back again—his gaze lingered at her chest for a split moment before saying, "Did we?"

"What?" Sage crowed, jumping off her bed. Realizing she was still in her navy-blue pajama pants and white tank top, she crossed her arms over her breasts. "Of course not."

Mason raked his fingers through his hair and glanced around the room. Sage cringed at her decor, suddenly embarrassed by her collection of colorful scrunch-ties lining her dresser, the row of identical purple boots underneath her bed, and the retro movie posters splattered on her walls.

"I...uh..." Mason took a hold of her bed frame, trying to keep his balance. "Why am I here then?"

All shame for her possessions vanished and she patted her bed. "You should probably sit down."

Mason's eyes drifted to her bicep. She followed his gaze to her own spiral mark. He sat onto the edge of her bed and rolled up his sleeve to reveal his mark. His long fingers traced the black on his skin. "You turned me, didn't you?"

"H... how?" Sage began, but her brain cut the question short as a million butterflies took flight inside her mind, bringing a million thoughts with them.

What she wanted to ask was how he could have possibly known that. But searching deeper, the question expanded. Because if he knew she'd turned him, then he knew what a Guardian was. Which meant, whoever marked him had told him about everything before marking him. That's how a True Guardian worked. That's what Makoto did for Sage. He explained everything before even asking her to become a Guardian.

As realization settled in, Sage sighed long and

loud. She didn't turn someone against their will... he was going to become a Guardian anyway.

Mason wandered over to the vanity, tilting his head as he stared deep into his own reflection. His hands curved over the back of the white chair, new muscles bulging beneath his torn school shirt. He took a quick breath out and nodded to himself. "This doesn't feel so bad."

Letting go of the chair, he rolled his shoulders back. "Actually, this feels damn good." He punched the air with both fists in quick succession. "Yeah."

Sage smiled to herself. She remembered that feeling well. A new vitality. Energy pumping through her very core. It was a great feeling.

Relaxing, she asked, "Why did Makoto mark you?"

"Who?" Mason teared his eyes from the mirror.

"Makoto? Why did he mark you?"

·  Mason shook his head. "Is Makoto a teenage girl with mood rings?"

Sage gawked at him.

His lips tilted into a smirk. "I'm joking, I know who Makoto is. I just don't know who marked me, all I saw was a hand on my arm. I was hoping the Shadow Society could help me, actually. Help me find a cure." His smile dropped as his eyes hit the mark on his wrist. "But you turned me instead."

"You?" Sage sprung up. If he didn't know who marked him, then it was most likely a Fallen. "You weren't marked on purpose?"

"'Fraid not." He waited a beat before adding, "Are you okay? You look pale."

"But how do you know about..." she hesitated, her brain racing to catch up.

"Guardians? The Veil? What the Shadow Society really is? How chickens fly?" Mason offered.

Suddenly light-headed, Sage reached for her bed. Trying to grasp something, anything, that would make sense. She licked her drying lips. With barely a whisper, she said, "Yes. All of it... except the chicken part."

Mason cupped her shoulders and led her backward. Sitting her down, he plonked himself beside her. Sage almost laughed at the absurdity of it. She thought she would be the one to steady him, not the other way around.

"Maybe you should have a rest. Catch up a bit. Okay?" Mason said.

Sage swallowed and nodded.

"All right. You do that." Mason tapped her knee as he pushed himself up and began for the door.

"W... wait!" Sage bounced to her feet again. "Where are you going?"

Mason shrugged and clutched her door handle. "What does it matter?"

The whole situation was not at all like she had imagined. No amount of conjured scenarios would have prepared for the reality. Sage rushed to the door and slammed her hand against it. "You can't just leave!"

"Why not?" Mason looked down his nose at Sage, his head hovering a good three inches above hers.

"You haven't answered my question. How do you know about Guardians?"

Mason squinted and a wry grin lifted his cheek bones. "Listen, I get you're probably a bit confused. Who becomes a Guardian if they haven't been selected by Makoto, right? But there's more of this life than the society. You know there're thousands, right? Has Makoto even taught you about the Fallen?"

The teasing tone in his voice infuriated Sage. She crossed her arms. "Yes, of course. Just answer the question."

The glint in Mason's eyes disappeared. Through clenched teeth, he said, "My dad is one. Happy?"

As he reached for the door again, Sage placed her whole body in front of it. "No. That just brings more questions. Many more questions." She paused for a moment and bringing a softer voice, she asked. "Is he a Fallen?"

"No." Mason scoffed, stepping back. "Rude! He is a True, just like you... or at least I thought you were. They don't normally turn people without their permission."

The vision of him bloodied and breathless on the wet gravel sent a pang of guilt flooding through her body. "What was I supposed to do?" she quivered. "You were dead."

"I was?" Mason seemed shocked. For a short moment, his cockiness washed away and standing before her was a broken boy, the same one she saw in the alley the night before. It didn't last long. A smirk fell over him again. "Well, I guess I should thank you, then."

Sage couldn't tell whether he was being serious or sarcastic. She had no time to find out as he brushed past her and opened the door. Running after him, she cried, "Wait! Where are you going?"

Still walking, Mason glanced over his shoulder. "Don't worry, I won't shift if that's what you're worried about. I'm just going to pretend this never happened."

"I don't think that's a great idea." Sage hurried beside him, trying to keep up. She couldn't let him leave.

A chuckle burst from Mason and echoed through the empty corridor. "Why are you so worked up? Relax a little."

Ugh. Sage frowned so hard she felt wrinkles set between her brows. "Uh, maybe because I just risked my place in the society to save you."

With a raised brow, Mason glanced at her sideways. Shaking his head, he said, "Don't worry your secret is so safe with me, I won't even let on that I've ever seen you."

That wasn't the point to Sage. He knew about Guardians and the Veil, but it was clear he didn't know everything. There was no way he could pretend his life was normal. He'd become a Guardian not a gardener. There was nothing flippant about the position he now held.

Sage followed him down the stairs. When they reached the ground floor and she was certain no one else was around, she said, "You know, if you leave it too long, your Guardian will become impatient. They might move forward while you're sleeping and take over and wander around without control."

Mason snorted. "That sounds like a myth."

"It's not a myth." Sage frowned. "Listen, I understand that your dad is what we are but that doesn't mean you can just waltz off without a care. There are rules you know?"

"Like what?" Without waiting for her answer, he added, "How to shift? What I'm protecting humans from exactly? Or just the basics like how to grow wings? 'Cause I don't think those things would suit my complexion."

Exasperated, Sage rolled her eyes. "You were better when you were half-asleep, you know that? And, don't worry, you won't be getting wings."

"Whatever," Mason shrugged, stopping near the double glass door entrance of the girl's dorm. "I guess I'm not a bird. Doesn't matter anyway, I'm not shifting. I'm not going to be a Guardian."

Sage stared at Mason's tiger as it stood beside him, encasing them both in a red aura. During the dormant stage, it may be easy for him to pretend to be human. Apart from the obvious heightened strength and senses, Mason was a measly human. But the longer he left the tiger waiting, the more impatient it would become. There was too much for her to teach him, it suddenly felt all too real and big.

"That thing before, about your Guardian taking over wasn't a myth, you know. Is your dad really a Guardian?"

Mason straightened. "Of course. Which is why I don't need your help. If it makes you happy, I'll go see him in July and he'll take me through it."

"That's five months away. I don't think you realize how important it is to get proper training, Mason."

Judgmental brows raised again as Mason glanced up and down her body. "And that proper training will come from a rookie who turns people without their permission? I'll take my chances on my own, thanks."

A heaviness fell over Sage. She had become responsible for a whole other person. What he did next, was a direct reflection on her. And he had no frickin' idea what the hell he was doing. This was going to be more trouble than it was worth.

"Maybe I should have just let you die then?" As soon as she spat the words, she regretted it.

Mason pushed his lips into a pout and nodded. "It's been... real," he said, facing to the door.

Sage's heart pulsed through her veins. At the end of her tether, she channeled her inner five-year-old and stomped her foot onto the linoleum. She half-shifted, eyes blazing purple and her wings spreading from her back. "Stop right there."

Mason paused. He took a quick breath, then turned with a wide smirk planted on face. "Tell me, rookie. What could *you* possibly teach me?"

"Well." Sage wriggled her shoulders as she returned to human form. "Firstly, there are the three main rules. Did Daddy Dearest tell you about them?"

Mason licked his lips and replied with a bored tone, "Uhh, as I said before not every Guardian comes from the precious society. So your rules may not be my dad's rules. Tell me yours and I'll let you know if mine are the same."

They were universal rules for all True Guardians. Sage ran them through in her head. Rules she had broken. She rubbed the nape of her neck. Maybe it would be best to let him go and do his own thing. If he ever said that she turned him it would be her word against his. And surely Makoto would believe her.

"So, no rules then? Great!" Mason said, impatiently turning around.

The tug returned. Burning a hole through Sage's gut. Ugh. No. She couldn't let him go. His strength unchecked made others vulnerable and she wouldn't be a part of that. Without training, without a clan, he'd be a rogue.

"What about the Fallen?" she tried.

A step through the doorway, Mason halted. "What about them?"

Encouraged by his hesitation, Sage pressed on, "Obviously one marked you. True Guardians always ask first. You've made it clear you know that. What if they attack you and you don't know how to defend or shift yourself?"

"Ha!" Mason blurted. He peered at his reflection in the double glass entrance doors and poked at his bicep. "I think I'll be okay. I'll make it to middle-weight division with these. Ben's gonna hate it." He glanced at Sage, letting his leering eyes give her body the once over yet again. Stepping out of the dormitory, he said, "See you around, I guess."

As the door swung shut, a slight gust of wind washed over her bare arms. Sage caught sight of her own reflection. She gawked at herself, still wearing her pajama pants and almost see-through white tank. Staring through the glass pane, she watched Mason march toward the boys' dorm.

It was a disaster. Camila was wrong and she was right. It was all her fault. A new Guardian was loose on campus and if he was left to his own devices, rogues often turned Fallen. He needed a clan.

In a last ditched effort, she pushed the door open and yelled, "Don't you want to know what animal your Guardian is?"

Half-way across the courtyard, Mason halted. His fists clenched at his sides for a beat. But before Sage could get any of her hopes up, he kept on walking.

# NINE

Sage missed most of her classes. She avoided the lunch time rush, too. In fact, she would have considered skipping the whole day if her next class wasn't with Makoto. Her absence would be too suspicious and the last thing she wanted was to draw attention to herself. So, with an uncertain heaviness, she dragged herself from the comfort of her dorm room and into the locker hall.

Facing Makoto worried her. Would she unconsciously give him reason to be suspicious of her? Would he see the secret hidden behind her fake smile? If he found out, for sure she'd be kicked out. Then what? Goodbye society. Goodbye Graystone. Goodbye Camila.

Hello Aunt Blaire.

Sage stared blankly into her locker, ignoring the bustle of students around her as they swapped their books for the next class. She hadn't seen her aunt since Christmas. The thought of returning made her heart sink.

It never used to be that way. After Sage's parents died when she was seven, the only thing that got her through was knowing she was going to live with her mother's fun twenty-two year old sister.

Aunt Blaire tried. Sage held onto that. At the beginning, they were comfort to each other in a time of immense pain. But quicker than either would like to admit, the obligation turned into resentment. Blaire wanted to travel, socialize, grow her business as an artist; and Sage's presence reminded her of all the things she couldn't have. And soon, Blaire stopped hugging Sage. She stopped telling her she loved her. She stopped saying, "everything's going to be okay."

Sage became an inconvenience. An unwelcome distraction. And when she could still smell the smoke from her thirteenth birthday candles, Sage found herself on the next bus from California to Washington.

Boarding school was a blessing. She'd found Camila. And even though she couldn't quite figure out the others, they were her clan. Her family.

Going back to her aunt wasn't an option.

She just needed to get through till the end of semester. She could graduate and pretend she turned Mason after. She'd have to convince him to train in secret, all while making sure all her classes were up to date so it wasn't suspicious. It was possible, she guessed, not truly convincing herself.

Sighing, she clutched her fake workbook and practiced her fake smile into the locker compartment.

*Everything's going to be okay,* she told herself, grabbing her locker door. *As long as Mason doesn't ruin everything.*

As she began to swing the door shut, a looming shadow caught the corner of her eye. Behind her locker door stood a boy almost six foot tall. His arms were crossed against his muscular chest, brown hair falling over emerald eyes. A tiny smirk lurked at the edges of his mouth.

"Hey, Guardian!" Mason boomed.

A shocked peep flew out Sage's mouth as she jumped back in surprise. "Mason! We can't say that in public," she scolded, glancing up and down the corridor. Not a single student was around.

He leaned in and whispered, "I think we're safe."

"You can never be too careful." As soon as the words left her mouth, Sage cringed. What was she? Seventeen or seventy?

As if reading her thoughts, Mason quipped, "All right, Grandma."

"What do you want?" she said, securing her locker.

"Well..." Mason winced and scratched his head. "I was kind of wondering what my..."—he paused to give a nervous chuckle—"What my Guardian is."

"I thought you didn't care about what you were. I thought you weren't going to be shifting." Sage tried to hold in the smug grin that pressed at her lips. But it was no use. She'd gotten through to him.

Mason's expression changed. As if he wasn't close enough, he took a step toward her. Imploring her eyes, he asked, "Was I really dead?"

"Yes." Her voice was so low she wasn't sure she even made a noise. She cleared her throat and repeated, louder, "Yes."

Mason nodded and moved back, leaning against Sage's locker. "Brothers, hey?"

The mood was too somber for his casual comment to land. An anger Sage had never felt before bubbled to the surface. "Brothers, what? Kill each other?"

The corridor fell silent. Mason's downcast eyes scared her. Had she scratched at the wrong itch?

Looking up slowly, Mason's gaze landed on Sage. "Are you going to tell me what my Guardian is or not?"

Two thoughts ran hand-in-hand through Sage's mind. The first one was that Mason was way too much for her to handle. And the second was that she had to help him. No, that she was the *only* one that could help him.

"Here's the deal," she said, rolling her shoulders back and straightening her blazer. "I'll tell you what your animal is, if you agree to let me train you."

Mason stared at her for a while, eye's turning into slits. A tiny smile made it way to his mouth. Nodding, he said, "You drive a hard bargain."

Before he could change his mind, Sage blurted. "Done. You're a tiger. Meet me after school."

She spun on her heels and marched down the corridor to the stairwell. He followed her.

"Sage, wait!" Mason called.

She stopped half-way up the stairs and stared ahead, waiting for him to come up with some kind of excuse as to why he didn't want to train.

He passed her and jumped to the step above her. "I wanted to say thank you."

"What for?" Sage knew exactly what for.

"For saving my life. I didn't want to be a Guardian but you're right, it's better than death."

Sage continued up the stairs. "Well, I didn't really do anything no other Guardian would."

Hurrying, to keep up with her, Mason said, "Exactly. To begin with I thought you jipped me. But now I see it's you who's got the raw end of the deal. I'm your burden to bear. I'm sorry."

Sage shrugged. The apology played at odds with her memory. She had to help him, and she'd do it all over again. "Don't be."

"I wish I could give you something in return."

"Like what?" she asked dubiously.

He thought for a moment, the two of them strolling down the school corridor like long-time friends. "How about some boxing lessons?"

Down the corridor, Sage watched the Shadow Society door get closer. She stopped walking and scrunched her nose. "I don't think so."

"I just think it's hardly fair that I get to be a muscular powerful tiger and you're a teeny little owl. What are you gonna do in a fight? Fly away?"

Sage tore her eyes from the door. She desperately wished she wasn't a teeny little owl and hated that he, along with everyone else, thought of her that way. She lifted her chin indignantly. "I can scratch. And, I'm very good at distraction." She watched his expression hoping he'd buy it. Because she knew she sure didn't.

"Uhh, no. You don't convince me. Come on." He smacked his palms together in plea. "You show me how to be an awesome Guardian and I'll show you—"

A nearby classroom door swung open and a student sauntered out. They took a second to study Mason and Sage before heading down the corridor in the opposite direction. The sounds of the teacher giving a lesson on history, drifted through the adjacent door.

Sage's throat went dry. She snapped, "You'll show me nothing."

"Why?" Mason looked hurt.

Clutching his wrist, she dragged him down the corridor. Whispering, she hissed, "I've just spent the last five minutes talking about something that shouldn't be spoken about in public. One minute you don't want a bar of this and the next you're being too cavalier about it all."

Mason wriggled his arm from her grasp. "I get it. I was shocked at first, all right? I'm suddenly something I never wanted to be. Excuse me for trying to make the most of it. Besides, no one was around, just chill a bit, yeah?"

Reality begun to sink in. She was well in over her head. It was too much. Sage felt her heartbeat pulsing in her eardrums. She needed to reel this in before he blew everything.

"It doesn't matter. No one can know about this. You hear me? No one. I think it's best for both of us if you don't talk to me."

Mason looked like he was about to start laughing right then and there in the middle of the school. "What, are you going to teach me to shift by mime only?"

Him being logical only served to infuriate Sage more. Her whole world felt like it was caving in around her and here this boy was making jokes. She glanced at the opened-door classroom, fingertips finding her temples. "I'll teach you the basics, one lesson on how to shift so your Guardian doesn't take over. But after that, no more activities, I can't draw eyes and spend more time with you."

"Aww. Come on, Bright Eyes," Mason urged. "We'll do boxing on Tuesdays at four. It's just an hour a week. Let me teach you to defend yourself."

The nickname gave her pause. Her mother used to call her that, before... Sage snapped. "Don't call me that. And I know how to defend myself."

"With more than just claws?" Mason asked, eyebrows raised.

"Talons."

"Whatever." He stood in front of her, grabbing her biceps and shaking her just a little. "Let me do this for you."

"Why does it matter so much? Just talking to you now is a massive risk for me. If anyone finds out you're a..." she glanced over her shoulder and back. "Guardian, my life here is ruined. I'm teaching you how to shift, then, we're done. You don't know me. I don't know you. Deal?"

"Okay." He stepped back, shoving his hands into his blazer pockets. "Message heard loud and clear. I won't even look at you." To that he snapped his eyes away from her and stormed down the corridor.

Sage watched him go, a pang tightening in her chest. If only that stupid instinctual tug would stop haunting her every time he wasn't near.

# TEN

Silence fell through The Shadow Society lecture room as Sage opened the door. All eyes were on her as she sheepishly walked inside. She was ten minutes late thanks to Mason and his ridiculous idea to give her boxing lessons.

"Nice to have you with us," Makoto said. "Everything all right?"

The excuse of not feeling well was out, Guardians didn't get sick. She panicked as he stared at her, waiting. "People," she blurted. "I... uhh... signed up for boxing."

Sage moaned internally. Did she literally just say that? They weren't the words she wanted.

"Boxing team?" Makoto glanced to Arielle. "Is this part of the assignment?"

"Uh." Arielle's light brown eyes went as wide as saucers. Despite Sage's wild nodding—a silent plea for Arielle to say yes and come up with some wonderful excuse that it was—she said, "No."

A nervous laugh fluttered from Sage's voice box. "No... it's not..."—she tugged on her mother's choker —"It was my own idea. I thought it might be handy. You know, if I ever bump into a Fallen, to have fighting skills. Owls can't exactly rip someone's throat out."

*Oh my God. Stop talking.* Sage scolded herself.

Makoto thought for a short moment, before saying, "Martial arts is part of our curriculum later in the semester, you know that right?"

Yes, she knew that. But nothing that made any sense was coming out of her mouth anyway so she went with a brain malfunction. "Uh..."

"But, why not?" Makoto shrugged, moving to his desk and finding a pen. As he scribbled on a piece of paper, he said, "I like your initiative. But make sure you don't miss any more classes because of it."

"Of course. After school only," Sage agreed, quickly finding her seat next to Camila.

Her best friend leaned over, lifting her hand to block those in front from reading her lips. "What is wrong with you?"

Sage could feel Nadya's eyes bore into her, she slumped into her seat until she couldn't see her anymore. "I guess you could say I've had an interesting day."

"Some success though?" Camila asked, hopefully.

"I think so." Sage tried to smile, but it was hard when she wasn't quite sure what success was supposed to look like. "Does this mean I have to take up boxing?"

Camila dropped her hand and chuckled. "Looks like it."

"Dammit."

After the bell rang, they recited the rules. Sage may have whispered the "I won't turn anyone until I graduate" one.

As they stood, Camila hooked her arm through Sage's. "Tell me everything."

Sage glanced at Makoto, gathering things from his desk and piling them into his drawer. She turned to

Camila. "I will. Just give me a minute. I'll meet you in the dorms."

Camila released Sage. "Oka—"

"Cami!" Arielle called, waiting near the door. She smiled brightly, eyes shining with hope and eagerness. "I've got a present for you."

"Ugh, she thinks we're besties all of a sudden. Swapping jewelry or something weird," Camila moaned. Then, she waved her hand at Arielle, and said sweetly, "I'm coming."

"Be nice." Sage swept her arm through Camila's. She whispered, "She means well."

As they started walking down the aisle, Camila curled her full lips. "That's the worst part. I'm afraid I'm going to spoil her sweetness with my sour."

Sage squeezed Camila's arm. "You're more sweet than you realize."

They parted near the door, Camila with a smile firmly planted on her face. She looked over her shoulder, and crowed, "Don't forget our catch up."

When the rest of the recruits had left the room, Sage took a moment to breathe. She turned to face Makoto. He was absent-mindedly swiping through his phone. There was so much she wanted to ask him but how to do it without looking guilty?

As though sensing her staring at him, Makoto glanced up. He placed his phone on the desk and took a step toward her. "Is everything okay?"

Sage smiled and took another breath. Fingers kneading into the hem of her blazer, she stepped closer. "Yeah. I'm just wondering... Are you sure it's a good idea for me to do boxing? I mean, if we are going to do martial arts I may as well..."

"No, it's fine." Makoto leaned on his desk and crossed his ankles. "I've always thought I should extend the time of those lessons anyway. And as I said, it shows great initiative. Go for it."

"Great." Sage feigned excitement.

Makoto waited. Sage felt his eyes stare through her

soul. As if he could almost see what she was hiding. Was she really that transparent?

"Is there anything else?" Makoto asked.

Sage hesitated. She couldn't exactly tell him the truth, not without knowing how he'd react. "Well, I was wondering. What would happen, hypothetically, if a rule was broken?"

Makoto's left eye twitched. He uncrossed his legs and leaned forward to be level with her eyes. His voice was raspy as he said, "Death."

Sage felt her heart lurch to her throat and back.

After seeing her shocked expression, he let out a bellowing laugh. "Sage, I'm kidding. It really depends on the circumstances. Whether it was malicious, like one of my students being a Fallen, or if it was a mistake."

His answer didn't reassure her. So, she asked, "What makes someone a Fallen?"

"Again, that depends." Makoto explained, "Theoretically, most people who are turned by Trues are Trues and Fallens will create Fallens. But I've seen a Fallen come from a True."

"I thought that whoever turned them makes them what they are."

"Not technically." Makoto rested his hands behind him on the desk and settled in. "Sometimes it's simply in their personality. It's why I'm choosy with who I turn and why I have a lengthy program here. I'd never choose someone with a mean spirit to become a Guardian, whether they'll be turned by a True or not."

Sage had always thought she was True because Makoto had turned her. She didn't feel Fallen, but how could she be sure Mason wouldn't be? He was a bully, loved fighting, and albeit charming, he seemed reckless. "And what if you make a wrong choice?"

"That's easy." Makoto stood, face falling. "I'd have to kill them."

"Ha!" Sage burst, laughing. "Good one."

Makoto's expression didn't waver. "Oh, that one

wasn't a joke."

Sage's laugh petered out. The look on his face sent shivers down her spine. She took a step back toward the door, as though distance would stop him from seeing right through her.

"Are you okay?" Makoto asked, following her. "Is there a reason you're asking?"

"Huh?" Sage checked over her shoulder.

Five steps to the door.

"No."

Four steps. Three steps

"I was just wondering."

Two steps.

One step.

"See you tomorrow."

# ELEVEN

The moment Sage slammed the door behind her, two bodies crowded in close. Caspar and Nadya loomed over her with judging eyes. Nadya with an arrogant smile.

"What's up?" Caspar asked.

Behind the door, Sage could hear Makoto's footsteps approach. Quickly slipping away from them, she said, "Nothing."

They followed her down the corridor, one on either side of her. Nadya's eyes turned to slits. "I can sense a change in you. I can't decide whether it's for the better, but there's a definite change regardless."

Sage didn't want to give her the satisfaction of being right. She shrugged. "I've got a lot on my plate, with the assignment and all."

They glanced at each other. Caspar crowed, "Yeah, a pee-wee nerd and a bully. Such a hard mission."

*If only they knew the half of it,* Sage thought.

"Nah, it's more than that," Nadya said. "You've done something."

Sage's fears had come to life. She gave herself away without even trying. Dropping into her best poker face—which consisted of a twitching cheek—

Sage said, "I really don't know what you're talking about."

As she sped ahead to her locker, Sage heard Nadya scoff, "Come on, Caspar. She doesn't trust us."

Caspar didn't seem to accept that. He rushed past Sage and held his hand against her locker, stopping her from opening it. He urged, "You can trust us, you know that? We're a team. We're supposed to be like a family."

Makoto had spoken about that before, countless times. He said most graduates end up forming a clan with one as the Alpha. They moved on from Graystone Academy and spent their lives doing assignments together, always looking out for one another.

The whole concept felt foreign to Sage. But something she so desperately craved. She gazed into Caspar's deep brown eyes, wondering if she should tell him the truth.

As if reading her thoughts, Caspar said, "If it's something you can't tell Makoto, maybe you could tell us?"

Nadya moved in close behind him, her hands cupping his shoulders. She nodded at Sage, the tiniest of smiles on her stone-cold face. For the first time, Sage felt like they truly cared about her.

Camila knew her secret, but maybe... maybe if the others did too, they could all help her. They could deal with it together. The burden a little lighter, Sage smiled with relief.

With a shaking voice, she said, "This is it for me, you know my story. My parents are dead. My aunty is god knows where. I'm meant to be a Guardian. If I don't have this, I have..." She stopped, spotting Mason at the end of the hall. His eyes hooded as he noticed her. Averting his gaze, he walked on. Sage returned her attention to Caspar and Nadya. "I have nothing."

Nadya groaned, eyes rolling up. "So dramatic. Just tell us what's wrong already."

Frowning, Caspar squeezed Sages shoulder. "I can

understand that. Listen, I know you were lost before all of this. I know how that's hurt you. My brother and I went through the system until we got scholarships here. I get it. But being a Guardian isn't all you have. Why do you think Makoto picked us? Because he saw something special in us. You're going to graduate."

No she wouldn't, not if the truth came out. Sage gave a quick smile, reversing her decision to tell them anything at all. She opened her locker and pulled out her overdue English essay. She didn't want to talk about her past and she didn't want to talk about the possibility of not graduating. Whether they were trustworthy or not, the conversation was over.

"I'm bored," Nadya huffed. "She's not talking. Are you coming, Cas?"

"Yeah," Caspar sighed, his sympathetic eyes boring into Sage. "Listen, I know we all have our differences but we're family. Whatever it is you've done or think you've done that is so wrong, we've got your back. I hope you know that."

As he ran to catch up to Nadya, Sage closed her locker. She watched the two of them, the perfect recruits, flounce towards the entrance. There was no way they'd accept her, not if they knew what she'd done.

Sage stood in front of her open closet, scanning her clothes. What did one wear to boxing lessons? She opted for some black stretch leggings and a dark blue tee-shirt with a cat floating in the milky way. She tied the bottom of the shirt into a knot on the side, turning it into a midriff. When Makoto turned her, toned abs appeared overnight. She felt proud and unworthy of them at the same time.

Facing her mirror, she pulled half her purple locks into a high messy bun. The only footwear she owned were her combat boots. Shrugging, Sage pulled them on. She stood back and looked over her outfit. It was absolutely not what one should wear to boxing lessons, but it was her, so Mason would have to deal with it.

She ran her hands down her thighs. *Right, first boxing lesson, here I come.* A gentle knock on her door interrupted her pep-talk. Sage opened the door to a wide-eyed Arielle.

"Oh thank the heavens, you're here." Arielle pushed the door and let herself in.

"Is everything okay?"

Arielle wandered to Sage's vanity dresser and picked up a blue and white striped scrunchie hair tie. "Mmm? Oh yeah. Just wanted to ask you how you went yesterday."

"Yesterday?" Sage asked, watching in horror as Arielle pulled her hair through the tie at the nape of her neck.

She turned sideways to look over her reflection, then ripped the scrunchie out and dropped it back onto the dresser. "With the bully. What was his name?"

Sage balked. It took her a beat to realize that Arielle knew she followed him the night before, not that she knew her secret. She cleared her throat and said, "Mason... I think."

"That's it. Mason. Did you witness anymore bullying?" Arielle plonked herself onto Sage's bed, tucking her hands under her thighs and looking at Sage with an innocent smile.

Playing it cool, Sage pulled her vanity chair out and swung it around. She sat down opposite Arielle. "Nah, I think you and Camila scarred him for life."

The freckles on Arielle's nose danced as she scrunched it in delight. She kicked her feet out. "I knew it! We were on point yesterday."

"Sure were." Sage appeased. "Is there anything else you wanted to talk about?"

Arielle dropped her feet to the floor with a thud.

Her bottom lip rolled out. "About Cami."

"What about Camila?" Sage asked.

A strange squeak vibrated in the back of Arielle's throat as though she was trying to find the right words. "I'm worried about her."

Sage leapt from her chair. "Where is she? Is she all right?"

"Oh, yes. She's fine," Arielle urged, standing up. "She's in the rumpus watching some odd game show."

"Takeshi's Castle?" Sage asked.

"Huh?"

"They have these weird games for contestants. They run across gauntlets with things being thrown... you know what? Never mind. Why are you worried?"

"Well..." Arielle dragged the word out, almost as if it were for dramatic effect. She looked at Sage with uneven brows, pensive sadness filling her eyes. "She's been saying some scary stuff. That she's bored with class. That she wishes we could tackle a real problem, like a..." Arielle lowered her voice, "Fallen."

"Oh that." Sage gave an internal sigh of relief. "She's always saying crazy stuff like that. It's just who she is. But she'd never actually break a rule."

Arielle grinned. "Yeah, of course. I didn't actually think she'd do something about it. Because that would be horrible."

"Yeah." Sage forced a smile. "It would be a disaster."

"Okay!" Arielle beamed. She bounced on her heels. "Did you wanna do something? Go watch this Kapecki's Castle?"

"Takeshi," Sage corrected, glancing at her phone. Mason had told her Tuesdays at four. She had ten minutes to get there.

Sage gently guided Arielle to the door and pushed her out into the corridor. "Actually," she said, closing the door behind her. "I've got plans."

# TWELVE

Underneath the broken neon sign, Sage took three quick breaths. She stepped into the studio, ready for her lesson. It was quiet inside, apart from the constant beat of fist against boxing bag.

In the corner, behind the ring, Mason was working up a sweat. He was shirtless and his hair was frayed and wet, sticking to his forehead. She really didn't want to spend more time with him than needed. But she had to show Makoto she'd learned something or he'd start to get suspicious. At least off campus no one at school could see her with him and attach her to his Guardian status.

She waltzed with confidence toward him. The moment he noticed her approaching, he grabbed the bag to stop it from swinging. "What are you doing?" he whispered, glancing across the room. "I thought you didn't want anything to do with me?"

Sage followed his eye-line and found Ben on the other side of the room stacking up weights. His face had three deep, red scratches curving around one side. She'd really gotten him good. Turning back, she said, "Firstly, I didn't say that exactly. And secondly..." She lowered her voice. "Why haven't you sent your brother to jail yet?"

It was a genuine question. Ben had tried to kill

him. If she hadn't been there and turned him, Mason would be dead. She didn't understand how he could even stand the sight of him.

Mason began unwrapping the bandage from his hands. "Okay, well. A, yes you did say that, and Z, my brother is none of your business. Why are you here?"

"You said it yourself. I'm a sad little owl."

Mason smirked. "Don't put words in my mouth. I never said you were sad. Anyway, what's that got to do with anything?"

Sage crossed her arms. This boy infuriated her. He knew very well what she was there for. "I thought we could do each other favors. You teach me how to fight and I teach you how to shift."

"Oh, what a brilliant idea." Still holding his bandage, Mason threw his hands in the air. "How ever did you think of it?"

She clenched her fist and threw it at the boxing bag. "Deal or not?"

Mason raised his eyebrows. "I got you, Flossy." He took her hand and peeled her fingers open. Then, he carefully placed them into a fist again, but this time he made sure to tuck her thumb against her palm. "Try that again."

Sage noticed Mason liked to give her nicknames. Grandma, Rookie, Bright Eyes—which was way too close to home—and now this odd one. Exasperated, she asked, "Why Flossy?"

Mason took a strand of her loose hair between his fingers and let it fall around her bun. "Because your hair is purple like cotton candy, or fairy floss. You don't like it?"

"Let's just keep it professional." She didn't like him getting familiar enough to dish out nicknames.

Sage licked her lips and thrust her arm forward, letting her knuckles hit the red vinyl. The bag moved toward Mason from the force. When she was done, she let her hand drop to her side.

"Not bad." Mason seemed impressed at her

strength. He moved around behind her. She felt the warmth of his chest near her back, close but not touching. He lifted her hands up and placed them in front of her face. His breath brushed across her cheek as he said, "Start from this position. Always protect yourself. When you hit, return your hand to this spot. Go again."

With Mason still behind her, she threw another punch, quickly whipping her hand to the bag and back. She looked over her shoulder, smiling. But Mason didn't see what she'd done, his eyes firmly on her face.

"Good." Mason's voice was low. He blinked and averted his gaze, a shy smile growing.

"What's this?" Ben said behind them.

Sage spun around. He seemed bigger during the day than the night before in the alley. He crossed his arms, causing his muscles to protrude in an unnatural way. Looking down his nose, he said, "You gonna introduce me to your girlfriend?"

Visions of the night before flooded her mind. His wild eyes and unmerciful blows against his own brother. The only thing that stopped her from launching at him was Mason tensing beside her.

"Ugh," he groaned. "Sage, this is my brother Ben. Ben, this is my *friend* Sage."

Ben released his arms and gave a slight nod. "Sage." He threw a thumb over his shoulder. "Mase, can I chat with you for a moment?"

As Ben walked through a door labeled "office" Sage tugged on Mason's elbow. "Are you sure?"

Mason gave a reassuring smile. "It's fine. He'll be cool. He always is after..." For the first time since she'd walked in, Mason's face dropped. He shook his head. "Don't worry."

She watched him enter the office and kept her eyes through the open door. They talked for a few minutes. Ben seemed remorseful, it even looked like he said sorry.

Mason walked back to Sage. She tried to hold herself together, but his casual demeanor didn't make any sense to her. She blurted, "I don't get it."

"What?"

"How can you forgive him for how he's treated you?"

Mason shrugged, trying to avoid her eye contact. "He's my brother."

It wasn't that simple. Sage knew that blood didn't always mean family. Heck, Aunt Blair hadn't ever laid a finger on her, but missed meals and lack of affection was enough to teach her that lesson.

"So, what?" Sage argued. "He says sorry and everything is suddenly fine?"

Mason squared his shoulders. With a glint in his eyes he asked, "You care about me, don't you?"

Sage gaped at his unexpected response. "What? No."

"What are you here for, Sage?"

It was a loaded question. She was there because the knot in her stomach pulled her there. She was there because she turned him. She was there because she accidentally told Makoto about learning damn boxing.

The creases between Mason's brows deepened as his eyes flitted between hers. She said nothing in reply, but he seemed amused regardless. He licked his lips. "Are we here to talk or trade lessons?"

He was right, in his own exhausting way. Mason and his brother may have issues. But she wasn't there to teach Ben a lesson, she was there for Mason. To make sure he became a True.

So, she gave a nervous smile and said, "Boxing. I'm here to box."

After Mason taught Sage the basics, he led her into

the ring. They stood toe-to-toe, hands up, elbows bent. Sage stared into his sparkling eyes. Mason was obviously a much more forgiving person that she was. The moment she stopped talking about his brother, he was a different person. He seemed to be enjoying teaching her, too. For a brief moment, Sage admired him.

A cocky smile grew across his face as though he knew what she was thinking. Confidence oozed out of him more than sweat. All at once, he reverted to his arrogant and annoying self.

"Now, your opponent may be bigger and more skillful but all you need to do is find their weakness. It could be that they are big but also slow. It could be that they are fast but pack a weak punch. You find their weakness and you've got your win."

"Yeah? What's your weakness?" Sage teased.

"I'm reckless," Mason stated. "Now, punch me."

Sage dropped her hands. "What?"

He tapped at her hands. "Keep 'em up. Hit me."

She raised her hands, wincing at the thought. He was irritating but nothing felt right about hitting him. She was meant to guide him, not hurt him.

Throwing a fist at his chest, Sage squeezed her eyes shut. Her knuckles landed onto something soft. She peeled her eyes open to see her hand cradled inside Mason's glove.

"Try again," he said. "This time, put some oomph into it... and keep your eyes open."

Sage nodded. She rolled her body, just like he taught her, aiming for his chest. When she saw his hand move to stop her, she quickly swung her other arm and jabbed him in the gut.

Mason stumbled back, hunching over. He lifted his head, groaning and staring at her in shock. Between breaths, he said, "Ugh... I did not... expect that."

Rushing forward, Sage grabbed his shoulders to steady him. She whispered, "I'm a Guardian remember, I'm strong."

"Mhmm." Mason threw his hand onto hers that held him. Catching his breath, he straightened. "I'll keep that in mind."

"You wanna take a break?"

Mason stretched his arms across his chest. "Actually, no. I'm fine."

Sage smiled. "You feel better already, huh? Just another perk, speedy healing."

"You know, Dad always talked about feeling invincible. I guess I never really understood that, until now." A childlike grin lit up his face. He ripped the velcro off his gloves and wriggled his hands out. "Can we go practice the shift now?"

"You've sure changed your tune from this morning. What made you change your mind? Why didn't you want to be Guardian then, but you do now?" Sage said, mirroring his cheekiness. She'd never tell him, but she was actually enjoying herself.

Mason glanced over his shoulder at Ben, who was lifting weights in the corner, headphones over his ears. He turned back to Sage and mouthed, "Him."

That wasn't an answer. So, Sage probed, "Why? Does he know I turned you and is excited to have you move up to middle-weight?"

"Huh?" Mason gawked. "No, I didn't tell him. Heck no. Why would I? Of course not. Anyway, you didn't answer, can we practice the shift now?"

Sage watched his face fold in on itself, contorting into at least five different expressions within a few seconds. She tried not to laugh. "What? Am I a pro already? I thought it was *my* lesson time."

Motioning to the large clock near the front door, Mason said, "Actually, your lesson ended over half an hour ago. But, I dunno, you're okay company, so..." He shrugged, emerald irises twinkling.

She turned to face the clock. It was already half past six—they'd missed dinner. Somewhere along the way, she'd forgotten that she had wanted to get this all over and done with as soon as possible.

70

The afternoon hadn't exactly turned out the way she thought it would, and she wasn't sure whether it was a good thing or a bad thing that she had liked it a little. But his cocky smirk and confident words—they weren't what she needed. She needed him to be responsible, to be serious, to be inconspicuous. But instead, he took things way too light-hearted, acting as though nothing mattered. As though he could act however he wanted and it wouldn't lead to complications. They weren't meant to become friends.

Sage ran a finger over her choker. It always seemed to calm her in moments of uncertainty. The rough yet soft leather against her skin, a second of clarity. She always saw her mother's face in that second, too. A warm smile. The last words she ever said to her: "I love you, Bright Eyes. Stay out of trouble."

Out of the corner of her eye she saw Mason move. He stepped through the ropes, then held them apart for her to follow. She bent down and took the hand he held out. As she stepped through the ropes and jumped out of the ring, she could sense his shining smile bearing down on her.

It mattered. She couldn't explain why. The way Mason smiled at her mattered. Spending time with him mattered. Liking both those things mattered. And the whole thing felt like a slippery slope.

"Okay, bye," Sage snapped, heading for the door.

Mason chased after her, his footsteps echoing on the floorboards. He ducked around her as she reached for the handle. Standing in front of her, he pushed his back against the door to open it.

"You wanna ride back?"

Sage cast her eyes on the bike in the parking lot. She let out a guffaw. Lifting her gaze to the darkening sky, she muttered, "I'd rather fly, thanks."

"Have I upset you?" he asked.

"No. Maybe." Sage met his gaze. "No. I'm just hungry, if I leave now I might find some dinner scraps before they chuck it out."

It was a lie. She wasn't hungry. She just needed some space.

"All right. I guess I'll see you tomorrow." He gave a soft smile. As she ran toward the forest, she heard him add, "Remember, Floss, no talking to me at school."

# THIRTEEN

Sage laid on her bed. Exhausted yet oddly exhilarated. Her phone dinged twice.

Two messages from Mason lit up the screen. The first one said: *You did good today. My turn tomorrow? Teach me all you know oh wise one.* It was followed by: *open your door.*

Sage sprung up and stared at her door. She gently pressed her feet to the floorboards and tip-toed across the room. As she reached for the door, it swung open.

Camila stood in the doorway, holding a wrapped burger from a local fast food place. She unfolded a note and pranced past Sage, reading, *"Sorry for making you miss dinner.* Who's this from?"

In one fell swoop, Sage closed the door and snatched the note from Camila. Mason's handwriting was messy but legible and had small round letters with long ends on the f and the k. Smiling she took the burger.

Camila collapsed onto Sage's bed. "Where the hell have you been—and what's with the creepy grin?" Her eyes darted to Sage's phone. She lunged across the bed and swiped the phone. "You're texting this dude now? And he bought you dinner? Oh girl, you are in so much trouble."

"It's not like that." Sage said, taking her phone back. "I'm teaching him how to be a Guardian and he's teaching me how to fight."

Camila rolled her eyes and pointed at the burger. "I told you. Trouble."

The way she said trouble, accentuating the "l" sound, reminded her of her mother.

"What have you been doing?" Sage said, changing the subject. She sat down on her chair and bit into the burger.

"Oh, yeah." Camila sat up again. "AJ? Our little nerd assignment? He's been marked."

Mouth full of bread, Sage blurted, "Say what?"

"Well, we will know for sure in a few days, but he's got the sickness. Sweats, sleeping, rash on his arm." Camila explained with a pout.

"And it wasn't Makoto?" Sage asked before taking another bite.

"Don't know, we haven't told him." Camila grimaced. "But I doubt it. AJ has no idea what's going on. He thinks he's dying. If it was a True that marked him, he would've been asked, you know?"

That was truth. Just like Mason didn't know who marked him. A shiver ran down Sage's spine. "Do you think there's a Fallen in this school?"

Camila clapped her hands together, her brown eyes widening. "Oh. Em. Gee. Wouldn't that be amazing?"

Sage opened her mouth to speak but shoved the rest of her burger in instead. She frowned at Camila and shook her head.

"Think about it." Camila slid to the edge of Sage's bed. "No more stupid piddly missions. Here's something of substance right in front of us. This will test us. Finally, something. Right?"

Sage swallowed. "I don't know. I'd rather know all I can first. Be all I can. Before I come face-to-face with a Fallen."

"Maybe you already have?" Camila gave a wild grin before standing up. Walking across the room, she mused, "Sometimes, we can only show our true colors when we are tested to our limits." She stopped at Sage's vanity and rested her hands on the dresser. As she stared at herself in the mirror, her eyes brightened. She glared at Sage's reflection. "Do you think we should turn him? Like you did with Mason, to make sure he's a True?"

Camila's enthusiasm was a little disconcerting. Sage offered, "Isn't there a cure, though?"

Turning around and leaning on the dresser Camila glowered. "That's all right for you to say. You've already got the opportunity to turn someone. What's it like?"

"What's it like?" Sage repeated, almost insulted at the question. The sight of Mason flashed through her mind. Blood streaming from his mouth as he struggled to breathe. "Camila, this isn't a game. It was scary. I had no other choice."

Camila nodded and turned to face the mirror again. "I get that and I'm sorry if I offended you. I just hope that if AJ needs to be turned, I get to be the one to do it."

Things were unraveling too fast. Just when Sage felt like she had the Mason situation under control, this whole AJ thing pops up. Not to mention Camila getting all obsessed about the Fallen.

Her voice cracked as she said, "If AJ needs to be turned, I feel like we have bigger problems ahead of us."

Camila pushed herself away from the vanity and sat on the bed opposite Sage. "This whole thing is changing you. I mean, you love to obey rules, but it's tearing you apart that you broke one isn't it?"

Sage exhaled through her nose, long and loud, as though she was expelling part of the burden. That was why she loved Camila, she was always there, ready to share the load.

"It freaking sucks."

Camila placed a hand on Sage's knee. "Tell me everything, don't leave a drop out."

The gesture transported her back to the moment Camila asked about Sage's past, why she was so desperate for somewhere to belong. It was hard for her, to talk about things. Reliving it all brought too much pain. Sage brought her feet up and crossed her legs, then put her face in her hands all but ready to cry.

"Don't do that," Camila scolded, whipping Sage's hands away. "That's not what friends do. You don't need to hide from me. Tell me."

Sage lifted her face and stared Camila square in the eyes. In that moment, she knew she was safe, that her best friend would carry some of the weight. In between tears and laughter, Sage told Camila the whole story, from Mason's drop-kick brother to him leaving the burger.

And when she was done, Camila had many things to say but Sage's favorite response was: "I'm so proud of you."

Camila wrapped Sage up in her arms and squeezed her tight for a quick moment. When she let go, she held Sage at arm's length, and shaking her shoulders every few words, she said, "There is nothing you can't deal with. You are stronger than you could ever imagine. I see it in you. Girl, you saved a boy's life! You're such a bad-ass—"

"Camila," Sage moaned.

"Uh-uh. Don't *Camila* me. I'm not leaving till you believe it. Say it, say I'm a bad-ass."

"You're a bad-ass."

"Pff, I know that." Camila poked Sage's knee. "But you gotta say it about yourself. Go on."

Sage sighed. She knew Camila well enough to know that she wasn't going to let it go until she gave in. With a tone that rivaled the drip of a leaky tap, she mumbled, "I'm a bad-ass."

The face Camila pulled was a mix between disgust and disbelief. Rolling her eyes to the ceiling, she said, "You can do better than that."

"I'm a bad-ass," Sage said it loud, and as Mason would say, with a little oomph.

Camila smiled and nodded. "That's it. One more time, so the people in South Africa can hear it."

Sage felt a fire ignite in her belly. She clenched her fists, resting in her lap and yelled, "I'm a bad-ass!"

"Yes, you are!" Camila yelled back, jumping to her feet on the bed. "What are you?"

Sage stood on her seat and jumped onto her mattress. "I'm a bad-ass!"

On the other side of the wall, Sage heard a muffled, "Shut up."

Giggling, she collapsed onto her bed. Camila fell beside her. There was nothing a good self-motivating shouting fest couldn't fix.

"Man, I love you," Camila said, rolling to her side. "And am so completely jealous."

Sage rolled to face her. "You'll turn someone soon. Even if it isn't till you graduate."

Camila curled her lip, then smiled. "I know. But sooner would be better." She dragged herself off the bed and headed for the door. "Good night, killer. I'll see your bad self in the morning."

"Oh, Cami," Sage said as Camila opened the door. "Just a head's up. You should probably stop saying things like that around our innocent Arielle, it might get you into trouble."

"Meh." Camila shrugged and faced Sage, leaning her head on the door frame. "It seems that trouble finds us anyway."

# FOURTEEN

Sage woke with a newfound confidence. After her chat with Camila, she felt much better about the whole situation and her ability to deal with it. She was even quietly optimistic that Mason would be easier to handle than she thought.

However, one minute into the Shadow Society class, that all changed. The other recruits were visibly uncomfortable, shifting restlessly in their seats under the dubious stares of Makoto. He sat behind his desk and looked around room, brow lowered. It was obvious that not everything was under control.

Makoto's eyes rested on Arielle. "Mission report?"

Arielle smiled nervously. "Oh, it's going great, sir. Yes. Perfect. Everyone is doing their job brilliantly. Couldn't ask for better team." For heavens knows what reason, she gave an extra cheesy grin and added, "It's been an easy task, really."

"Is that so?" Makoto raised his brow. He took a moment to stare down the other four. Tapping his pen on the edge of the desk, he asked, "And how does everyone find Arielle as a leader? Camila?"

"I'm loving it!" Camila replied. Sage believed her.

Makoto cleared his throat and turned his attention

to Sage. "What do you think?"

"She's great," Sage blurted. "Great. Just..."

"Great?" Nadya answered for her.

Makoto leaned forward. "And what are your thoughts Nadya? Last time you were the mission leader and we closed the assignment within two hours. How do you think Arielle and the team are stacking up in comparison to last time?"

Nadya licked her lips and tilted her head thoughtfully. "You know I don't like to compare missions as they are different people in different circumstances. But all in all, I think we are doing the best we can." To end her statement, she gave two thumbs up accompanied by an uncharacteristic grin.

Makoto stared at her for a beat before looking at Caspar. "Would you agree?"

Caspar nodded quickly. "Yes, sir."

Makoto stood up, his chair legs scraping on the floor. After meeting the eyes of all five recruits he said, "All right. If you're happy with how its progressing, I'll leave it in your capable hands. Now, onto today's theoretical lesson: the cure for the mark."

Camila moaned.

After a long morning listening to Makoto, Sage sat in the courtyard with her lunch tray. The day's special was chicken Caesar salad. Ravenous, she chowed down.

"I love how easy the cure is," Camila said, taking a spot next to Sage. "Vervane and the blood of the one who marked them. Simple."

Nadya slid onto a seat opposite them. Scowling, she hissed, "Except how can we use the blood if we don't know who marked him,"

Sage looked up, surprised to see the perfect Guardian join their table. Directly behind Nadya, on the other side of the courtyard, two eyes watched them. Mason leaned against the brick wall, thumb running over his bottom lip. A small smile lit his face as Sage's eyes found his. He wriggled his fingers in a wave.

Caught between wanting to shoo him away and waving back, Sage gave the air an awkward swat. As she did, Caspar took a seat next to Nadya. He frowned and spun around, trying to spot who she was motioning to.

"It was a fly," Sage said, urging Caspar to stop looking.

It didn't matter anyway, Mason had already begun walking off.

"This is a bit suspicious don't you think?" Camila glared at Nadya. "We never hang out."

Caspar relaxed and faced the table again. "Well, maybe we should start. Maybe we should start acting like a family, too."

The way he said it sounded so righteous to Sage. It immediately rubbed her the wrong way. Before she could think better of it, she glowered, "Maybe we should have been doing that from the start... not when things got complicated?"

From the beginning of their training Nadya had distanced herself from them, as though she was too good to even speak to them. She dragged Caspar along for the ride and he was more than happy to follow, shunning everyone else along the way. Camila and Sage, and even Arielle, didn't seem like they'd ever be enough. But now, when things got rough, they wanted help.

"Fair call," Caspar muttered into his food.

With a lifted chin and no warmth in her eyes, Nadya said, "Well, we're here now."

Arielle dropped her tray onto the table and slid in on the other side of Camila. "Oh my... how the heck did we get out of class alive like that? I thought Makoto was onto us for sure."

Nadya rolled her eyes and picked at her salad, throwing bits of cheese to the side. "You're lucky I didn't tell him."

"Thank you," Arielle said, placing her hand on Nadya's shoulder. "We just need a bit of time, that's all."

"I feel sick." Nadya shrugged Arielle off and pushed her tray into the middle of the table.

"What's wrong?" Arielle picked up a lettuce leaf. "Is there something in the food?"

Sage covered her mouth, trying not to laugh. She couldn't believe how naive Arielle was sometimes. "I think she's talking about AJ being marked."

"Oh." Arielle gave a sheepish grin.

"There has to be a Fallen on campus," Nadya said, glancing around the courtyard. "And we're just here twiddling our thumbs."

Camila waved a fork in Nadya's direction. "Exactly. We need to find them."

Nadya met Camila's gaze with an icy stare. It was a show down between two of the strongest willed humans Sage had ever met. Nadya softened, nodding in agreement. It was probably the first time they'd agreed on something.

And that would have been great and all, if the task at hand wasn't completely out of their depth.

"And how do we find a Fallen?" Sage asked.

"Easy," Caspar said, stabbing a fork into Nadya's discarded cheese. "From the trail of the dead they leave."

Arielle shuddered.

Nadya whipped her head to him. "Does it have to come to that? Surely, there's another way."

"We could ask AJ who he came into contact with?" Caspar suggested. "Make a list then follow the lead?"

"Yes! That's brilliant," Sage said, slamming her palms onto the table. She hadn't even asked Mason who had touched him in the lead up to being marked. If she narrowed it down and cross checked his list with the list they get from AJ... then, they could find the Fallen who marked them both. The thought both exhilarated and terrified her.

"Let's do it!" Nadya declared, standing.

"I'm in," Arielle said, bouncing up.

Caspar quickly shoved the rest of his lunch into his mouth, and muffled, "On it."

"I'll meet you guys in the dorms." Camila's voice was a little softer than normal.

As Nadya, Caspar, and Arielle rushed off, Camila stayed seated, playing with her salad.

Sage gave Camila's shoulder a nudge on her way to her feet. "Come on, why so slow? You could find your very first Fallen."

Camila nodded, head close to her tray. "I'll catch up."

Sage straddled the seat and peered around to meet Camila's gaze. "I thought you'd be excited about this?"

"I am." Camila swallowed and shoved a piece of chicken in her mouth. "I just need to be nourished, you know. Enough energy to beat a Fallen."

Shaking her head, Sage collected her tray. "Okay, I'll put this away and wait for you inside."

She hurried toward the cafeteria, wondering what on earth had gotten into Camila. As she stepped through the doorway, she glanced over her shoulder. Camila raised her fork in a friendly wave, but her eyes told a different story. Sage couldn't decide whether it was fear, sadness or concern.

A sudden jolt forced Sage back into the courtyard. She stumbled. Her feet tripped over uneven cobblestone and her knees slammed onto the hard stone. Her tray skidded along the ground, small bits of uneaten lettuce scattering around it.

"Watch where you're going," a voice barked.

Bright blue trainers stood on the ground beside her. She traced the body they belonged to, from the un-ironed gray slacks to glaring green eyes and unbrushed hair.

Mason glowered down at her and whispered, "Play along."

The last thing she wanted to do was *play along*. She'd had her fair share of pretending already. Plus, contact at school wasn't part of their deal.

She dusted herself off and rose to her feet. Checking around for any onlookers, she hissed, "What are you doing?"

"I just want to make sure we're still on for today?"

"You could have texted." Sage gathered her tray and stepped to pass him.

He grabbed her elbow, clutching tight enough she felt it in her bones. "I wasn't sure you'd text me back. Did you get your dinner?"

"Yes." Sage winced, wriggling her arm out of his hold. "You're hurting me."

His face dropped, all color washing away. "Shit, sorry. I forget my strength sometimes."

"Just—" Sage stopped talking as Mason ran a thumb around her elbow. As his concerned eyes studied the marks his fingers made, she cleared her throat. "I'll heal."

It didn't seem to appease him. "Sorry," he said again. His thumb remained on her arm, grazing back and forth right below her elbow. "It doesn't matter if you'll heal. I don't want to hurt—"

"Are you okay?" Camila asked, taking the tray from Sage.

Seeing Camila, Mason's face folded in on itself, irate wrinkles forming between his eyebrows. He scowled, "Tell your clumsy friend to watch where she's going."

Eyes began turning to them, students whispering amongst themselves. That was it for Sage. Causing a scene was definitely not part of their deal.

She grabbed Camila, and as she rushed past Mason, she whispered, "I'll meet you after school."

As they entered the cafeteria, Camila let out a chuckle. "He's a terrible actor. Pretending to bump into you just so he could talk to you."

Sage shook her head and sighed.

"Oh my god." Camila glared at Sage, finger pointing inches from her face. "You like him, don't you?"

"I do not," Sage said the words quickly before ripping the trays out of Camila's grasp and placing them on the serving counter.

"I can see it in your face," Camila said right behind her. "You turned a boy and now he's your responsibility."

Of course he was her responsibility. There wasn't much that Camila did to annoy Sage, but making light out of something heavy was her worst trait. As she brushed past Camila, she growled, "You don't know what you're talking about."

Camila caught up and playfully locked their elbows together. She tugged Sage in close and whispered, "Plus, everyone loves the bad boy come good."

"He's not bad," Sage argued. "Just misunderstood."

Camila's laugh echoed down the corridor. "See."

# FIFTEEN

By the time Sage and Camila had gotten to AJ's dorm, Caspar, Nadya and Arielle were leaving.

Nadya held a piece of paper in her hand and closed the door. Seeing Camila and Sage she waved the paper. "He's in the delirious stage. We couldn't get much out of him."

"Not very helpful," Arielle said, snatching the piece of paper and shoving it in Camila's face.

Sage peered over Camila's shoulder to see. Three names were scrawled in Nadya's cursive handwriting.

*Arielle*
*Camila*
*Mason*

Sage's heart flipped. There was no way she would let them chase that lead down. She scoffed, "Well that's a dead end."

"Not exactly." Nadya tapped on a name. "Who's this Mason guy?"

"He's the bully, remember?" Caspar said, looking down the corridor. "I could find out his room number?"

Sage took a step forward to nowhere in particular. She had to move, she had to stop this before they followed that path. Almost spitting the words, she shouted, "He's not a Fallen."

Nadya staggered back, frowning at Sage's urgency. Her eyes turned into slits. With that go-to judging face Sage knew so well, Nadya asked, "And how would you know?"

Glancing at Camila, Sage said, "After we saved AJ from him, I followed him to make sure he didn't hurt anyone else. I looked at him, you know, with my eyes." Sage half-shifted, quickly flashing her eyes purple, and returned to human form before her wings could sprout. Even though she knew she'd already put too much into his defense, she emphatically added, "He's not a Guardian, he's not a Fallen."

The lie left a bitter taste in her mouth. From the glare Nadya gave, it almost seemed like she knew it was a lie, too.

Camila scrunched the paper into her fist and tucked it into her blazer pocket. "There has to be more people on this list, we need to wait until he's awake properly."

"I think so, too," Arielle piped up. "And, as the leader, this is what I suggest. Around the clock protection. We each take turns sitting with AJ. It would only be five hours each day. Then, at least, we can see if anyone is lingering around and we'll know when his mark appears."

Caspar raised his brow as though shocked and impressed. "That's actually a really good idea."

"Yeah," Nadya said, relaxing her stone-cold expression. "I agree."

Arielle beamed with pride. "Good then, it's settled. I'll do the first shift."

Sage should have been relieved that Mason was no longer the prime objective, but it was too close a call. His name was on the list and eventually, knowing Nadya's stubbornness, that path would be explored.

As though sent from the heavens, the bell rang to signal that lunch was over.

"Better go, class starts soon," Sage declared, spinning on her heels and bolting down the corridor.

"Be cool," Camila hushed, as they rushed across campus. "Your nerves will be your unraveling." She pulled at Sage to slow down. "Now chill, and tell me... what are you?"

Sage slowed her walk. And through gritted teeth, she said, "I'm a bad-ass."

As the final minute of the last class ticked over and the bell rang out, Sage remained at her science prac table. Vials of hyrdogen peroxide and potassium iodide foamed in front of her and she stared at the bubbles, wishing the time away. Her aim was to avoid Nadya and Caspar. Their spying eyes were not wanted, especially when she was supposed to meet Mason.

After the clattering of footsteps in the corridor petered out, Sage made her way out of the classroom. She peered down the hall toward the lockers and decided to turn the opposite direction. Her science prac book was going with her to her dorm room today. She slunk out the building's back exit and ran around the field toward the dorms.

Slowly sneaking around the back of the boys' dorm, she eyed the girls' dorm main entrance, checking for any sign of long platinum hair and steel eyes. Girls rushed in and out but no Nadya. She took sight of the fire escape along the far left wall. Her room was on the second floor and only two doors down from the fire escape window. A much safer option. She stepped out from behind the boys' building.

"Whatcha doing?"

Sage spun around, fists already clenching. When her eyes landed on Mason, she relaxed. He was dressed in a casual black hoody with ripped jeans and those stupid bright blue shoes. And if she was being honest with herself, he looked nice. Hitting his shoulder gently, she said, "Don't do that. I almost had a heart attack."

Mason smiled, amused. "Sorry. But seriously, what are you doing? You look a little stalker-ish."

"I'm trying to avoid someone... Nadya." Sage backed herself against the wall, taking a quick peek around the corner. Turning back, she explained, "She's been asking questions about you. I just wanted to sneak into my dorm without bumping into her."

"She's been asking about me?" Mason pointed to his chest, puffing up with pride.

"It's not a good thing." Sage glowered.

"Okay." Mason shuffled to the wall beside Sage and his green eyes sparkled down at her. "So, we shouldn't be seen talking here then?"

Sage tore herself away from his gaze. "Probably not."

Mason moved closer, his head hovered to the side of hers as he looked in the same direction. At the girls' dorm. "Want me to watch your six while you run between buildings?"

There was something about his proximity which made her nervous. And not in a 'getting caught seen with him' kind of way, more in a 'he made her feel vulnerable' way. Without looking at him, she nodded and made a run for it.

She bypassed the entrance and ran around the side to the fire escape. Entering on the second floor, she was careful to check that the hallway was clear before making a dash to her room. She'd gone two steps before her name was called.

"Sagey?" Arielle cooed.

*It could be worse,* Sage told herself as she turned around.

Arielle tapped her watch. "Are you right to start your shift in half?"

"Shift?" Sage asked, confused.

"For AJ? We need to keep watch on him, remember?" Arielle said. She gave a sympathetic smile. "You're not really all in with the assignment, huh?"

"Oh, right. Sorry. I forgot." Sage grimaced, trying to think of an excuse.

Arielle gave a sympathetic smile. "You want me to cover it for you?"

"Are you sure?" Sage asked, scanning the corridor. "I really do have things I need to do."

Waving her hand, Arielle said, "Don't even think twice about it. I'll do two shifts, three even. I'll stay round the clock to make sure he's safe."

The words gave Sage pause. She'd been so wrapped up in her own mistakes, she never stopped to consider Arielle would be feeling the same. He was marked under her watch. "You're amazing."

"No, you are." Arielle pointed at Sage as she began walking backwards. She lifted her chin and yelled down the corridor, "Everyone, Sage is awesome."

The volume on that petite girl was loud enough to wake a deceased dinosaur buried twenty feet below the ground. With eyes turning toward her, Sage ran to her room and swung the door open. She collapsed against the door, closing herself inside. She'd made it.

Sage changed into her favorite outfit—light blue denim overalls and a white tee. She pulled her boots on and checked herself in the mirror. Long scruffy purple locks wouldn't do for a training session. She tied her hair into two side braids to tidy it up a bit. Pausing for a moment, Sage frowned at her reflection and wondered why she was worried about how she looked. It was only Mason. She leaned forward and brushed a swoop of foundation powder over her face.

Leaving the building the way she entered, Sage clambered down the fire escape. Alert and taking in every face that surrounded the area, she ran back to where Mason was. As she approached him, her pace slowed.

He had half-shifted. In public. He was facing the wall with his claws out, scraping into rendered brick.

"What the hell are you doing?" Sage scolded.

Mason jerked his head around, eyes glowing red. He opened his mouth as if shocked to see her and his fangs popped over his bottom lip. He blinked and returned to human form.

"It's okay," he said, peering over her shoulder. "No one is around this side."

"That's not the point. If I could see you, anyone else could have," she huffed.

This boy was exhausting. He couldn't stick to her rules. He was always too casual about everything. And his smile made her feel things she'd rather not be feeling.

Mason gave an appeasing grin, like a middle grader who'd been caught putting slime on the teacher's chair. "I thought you'd be proud of me for teaching myself how to do it."

Sage felt her mouth drop open. She'd been so worried about him getting caught, she'd forgotten she hadn't taught him yet. Not many people were able to do that without instruction. "H... how?"

A sheepish smile hit his face. "Well, I got to thinking about what you said, about the Guardian taking over if I don't control the shift. So, last night I kind of forced myself to sit until I felt the tiger close and called it forward, but not too far forward. Enough to grow fangs and claws. And I practiced it all night until it became a second sense."

"Wow. That was quite responsible of you."

Mason rolled his eyes. "Is that shock I hear in your voice?"

Sage shrugged.

"Well, it wasn't all you," Mason continued. "It reminded me of this time with my dad. He had to go on some assignment, he muttered something about his clan member getting loose and I never really understood it until you mentioned that."

Sage nodded. "I'm not shocked by the way—" She stopped talking when Mason raised his eyebrows. "Okay, just a little. I'm glad you took the initiative. It makes me a bit more relaxed about things."

"Good." Mason took a few steps to his bike and held out a helmet. "You ready?"

She stared at the offering, then at the bike, then at him.

"What? You've never been on one before?" Mason asked before starting the engine.

"I usually fly."

"Right." He cocked his head toward the girls' dorm. "Does this Nadya girl have white hair and a resting bitch face?"

Sage darted her eyes to the entrance of the girls' dorm. Nadya was sitting on the front steps, talking with Caspar. As Nadya shifted her gaze, Sage grabbed the helmet and shoved it on her head. Mason held his hand to help her on, but she didn't have time for that. She leapt on behind him and yelled, "Go!"

And as she glanced back, her eyes wandered to the place where Mason was scraping with his claws. A small carving had been etched into the clay-like wall—the face of a barn owl.

# SIXTEEN

The ride wasn't very long but it was uphill and winding. Trees became a blur as they drove deeper into the forest. And Sage couldn't have loved it more. She sat behind Mason pressed up to his back, hands gripping his waist. She threw her head back and closed her eyes.

It almost felt as free as when she flew, but different somehow. Giving up control and putting her life in someone else's hands went against all she stood for. Yet, the thrill of it zipped through her being as though something dormant inside was awakening.

As the bike rolled to a stop and Mason climbed off, Sage fell to earth with a thud. Her mother's last words rang inside her mind, banging on the cages she'd built for herself. *"Stay out of trouble."*

"Why aren't we at the studio?" she asked, removing the helmet. "I thought you said Wednesday was your brother's day off."

"It is. But he's sick. And he gets cranky when he's sick. Besides, what's wrong with this place?" Mason took the helmet from Sage and clasped it to the back of his bike with a clip. Without waiting for her answer, he walked to the end of the path and into the forest.

Sage ran to catch up, stepping over twigs and old

leaves and pushing herself through branches that seemed to reach for her. As the trees gave way, a small clearing appeared. Sage found Mason standing at a cliff edge, a valley of rolling hills and scattered cabins beyond him.

"This is beautiful," she gasped.

Mason turned around—his eyes glowed red and fangs popped from between his lips. He studied her, eyes tracing her body. "I know."

She stared back at him. At his earnest face. And for one moment she allowed herself to acknowledge that he was growing on her.

But how could the face that looked at her like that also be the same face that scowled at AJ as though he was the scum of the earth? It didn't add up. There was something she didn't know about him.

The thought hit her all at once. He was pretending. But with her or with AJ? Makoto had always said that the Fallen were great at deception.

Could Mason be a Fallen? The thought made her stomach churn. She blurted, "Why were you teasing AJ?"

"What?" Mason's face dropped.

"In the library. You were bullying him."

"Oh that." He grinned and pointed to himself. "C'mon, look at this face. Is this the face of a bully?"

Sage glared.

"Fine," Mason sighed, defeated. "I just wanted to bring attention to myself. AJ seemed to be an easy target. And that boy in the corridor? I saw you close by and just grabbed him."

Sage was horrified. "You used those poor boys to get the society's attention?"

Mason shrugged. "It worked didn't it? For you, at least."

"Yes, but if you knew I was a Guardian why didn't you ask for help instead of playing games?"

Mason wondered to a boulder at the edge of the clearing. He sat down and ran his hands down his thighs. Staring at his knees, he said, "I was scared. I didn't know who to trust. It could have been a society member that marked me. The last thing I wanted was to be turned."

"Why?"

Looking up, Mason winced. "It's a lot, you know? That was Ben's dream. But after Dad told him his personality was too unstable... I just. I couldn't want it. Out of solidarity."

Sage recalled Mason telling her that he changed his mind about being a Guardian because of his brother. "Is that why Ben was mad and hit you? Because you'd been marked and he hadn't?"

Mason lifted his eyes to the clouded sky. "You know, I've carried this guilt for a long time. My dad always went on about how I'd make the perfect Guardian. In front of Ben, too. So, I told Ben not to be jealous, that it wasn't the life for me... that I didn't want it anyway."

"But you did want it?" Sage asked, creeping toward him.

Mason's tongue rolled around inside his mouth. As a gust of air danced through the forest behind them, Mason sighed and whispered, "Maybe."

"And now?" She knew the answer to that question already. He loved it, she could tell.

He let his gaze drop, his eyes bypassed Sage and fell to the ground. "I feel invincible."

"You kind of are." Sage tapped the end of his shoe with her boot.

A smile crept across his face. With his eyes still low, he returned the toe tap and asked, "Do you still think I'm a bully?"

"You want to know the truth?" Sage took a seat beside him. "I never really believed you were."

Mason's head shot up. Grinning, he nudged her with his elbow. "I knew you cared about me." Before she had a chance to protest, he leapt to his feet. "Well, I hope I didn't scar AJ for life."

Sage felt all color leave face.

Mason frowned. "I haven't traumatized him, have I?"

"No. It's just." Sage stood, giving herself a moment to decide whether to tell him or not. But before she'd finished mulling it over, the words were already out of her mouth. "He's been marked."

"What?" Mason gaped, eyebrows rising. "Are you serious?"

Sage nodded, giving a sad smile. "We're keeping a vigil outside his dorm, to look for any suspicious activity. But Mason... Maybe the person who marked him, marked you, too. Do you remember anything about what they looked like?"

Mason was quiet for a while. Thinking. He walked to a low branch and broke off a hanging twig.

Rolling the pencil-like piece between fingers, he mused, "There's a club in Burrville. A kind of secret dive bar underneath the old brewery. Apparently, it's a hot spot for Guardians—a place where they meet to relax and talk about the Veil and assignments. Last week, Ben wanted to go and find someone to mark him. Knowing what Dad said about him not being right for a Guardian, I freaked out. So, I told him I'd go instead, to check it out."

"And that's where you got marked?"

Mason dropped the twig and stepped toward Sage.

"It was crowded." He moved beside her, both of them facing a different direction. He took hold of her wrist, placing his fingers on her skin, one-by-one. "I felt someone do this." Sage looked down. "I saw delicate fingers with red painted nails and a mood ring on their thumb. Then, as quick as she touched me, she let me go." He whipped his hand away. "And by the time I thought to look at her face, all I saw was brown wavy hair flaunting toward the exit."

Sage ran her own fingers over the place that Mason had held, and said, "I wonder if it was the same person who marked AJ. Did she seem like a teenager?"

"I don't know." Mason shrugged. "Honestly, I didn't even realize I'd been marked."

It seemed like such a brazen act to Sage, for someone to mark another person so boldly in a place meant for sanctuary. She watched a darkened cloud make way for the sun. Squinting at the brightness, she mused, "A Fallen at a place for a True."

"They are good at deception," Mason said.

Another cloud rushed in, replacing the one before it—the brief moment of sunshine gone. "So I've heard."

Mason moved next to her and let his eyes follow the same direction she was gazing. He bumped her with his elbow. "So, Floss. You'd better get teaching before we miss dinner again. You say there are rules?"

"Right." Sage blinked a few times, snapping out of her daze. They were there to make sure Mason got a handle on the shift, not hang out and chat about other things. He distracted her so easily. She faced him and held up her index finger. "Rule one is not to show your true self to civilians. So, no shifting in broad daylight or on campus."

Mason's lips twitched into a lop-sided smirk. "Like you did in the library... and locker hall... and outside the studio?"

Sage pressed her pointed finger onto his chest. Seeing his cheeky grin, she sighed. "Correct. Not like that."

"And rule two?"

"The second rule is: don't kill anyone unless they're... no, you know what, just don't kill anyone."

"Sounds easy enough. And the third?"

"The last one is." Sage paused. Grimacing, she said, "Never turn anyone until after graduation..." She held up her hand in surrender. "Don't even."

"Wasn't going to say anything." Mason ran his finger over his mouth and threw an invisible key over his shoulder. He pursed his lips as though fighting to contain his amusement, but a smile crept into his eyes and gave him away.

"Don't!" Sage warned, trying not to laugh.

Mason cleared his throat and smoothed his hands down his hooded sweater. Then, with eyes turning into rubies, he said, "Can you teach me how to do the full shift now?"

Mason pulled the motorbike to a stop at the bottom gates of the school. The gates were made of old stone, older than the academy itself. Curved walls reached toward a gothic arch with a lion's head in the middle. A lantern hung beside the opening.

Mason helped Sage with her helmet and said, "I thought it might be a good idea to get back on campus separately. You know, so we don't raise suspicion."

Sage climbed off the bike. "Well, aren't you becoming a responsible human being? I'm so proud."

"Ha. Ha." Mason jeered. "Very funny, Grandma."

Shaking her head, Sage turned toward the forest edge. She'd decided to avoid the gates altogether by walking up the hill through the trees and making her way casually out near the dorms. As she took a step, Mason's hand cupped her shoulder.

"Actually," he said, urging her to turn around. "I was wondering if you wanted to meet up later?"

"Oh." Sage glanced through the arch and up the hill to the lights of the rec hall. Students bustled in and out, serving themselves spaghetti or lasagna or fried rice. Her stomach rumbled.

"After dinner," Mason confirmed, as though sensing her hesitation. He quickly added, "It's okay if you don't want to."

*Stay out of trouble.* There were her mother's words again. She lifted her hand, fingers moving for the old leather necklace. Before she could touch it though, she snapped her hand to her side. The more time she spent with Mason, the less she felt inclined to heed her mother's final words.

Still looking out to campus Sage rolled her eyes at her growing likeness for this boy. "What did you want to meet up for?"

"Well, now I'm a Guardian it's my job to protect innocents from Fallen right?"

Sage fell back down to earth. He'd done a full shift twice during practice and now he's an expert? Slowly facing him, Sage cautiously said, "Right, but there's more to it than—"

Without letting her finish, Mason interjected, "I need to find this person who marked me and AJ. I need to take them down before they turn AJ. Or *we* do, together."

"No, no, no." Sage bristled. "Not so fast, Bucko."

"Bucko? Find something original, Fairy Floss. Besides, we know the location, where they hang out. All we have to do is just look at hands and hair. How hard can it be?"

Sage couldn't believe what she was hearing. "You want to go to this bar? Where swarms of Guardians sit and drink? Guardians that could be True or Fallen? And imagine, seriously, just imagine that this Fallen who marked you is there and sees you. That's asking for trouble."

Mason nodded. "Yep."

Sage gawked at him. She waited for him to start laughing at tell her it was a joke. But he didn't.

"So," Mason asked. "What's your answer?"

"You're absolutely crazy. We can't just march into this place. My answer is no." Sage swiveled on her heels and as she headed for the forest, she muttered to herself, "The nerve of him. Thinks he's king shi—"

"Okay," Mason called after her. "I'll let you know how I go."

Sage skidded to a halt and spun around. The last rays of sun flickered across the ends of his hair, giving him a golden halo. "What does that mean?"

Mason gave his signature arrogant smirk and

started the engine. "It means that I'm going anyway. Whether you come or not is up to you. Nine o-clock, outside the boys' dorms."

He sped through the archway. As she heard the sound of his motorbike wind up the driveway toward the dormitories, Sage stormed into the forest. Infuriated, she shifted with her owl. How dare he manipulate her like that. He wasn't going to win that one, there was no way she could agree to going to that place.

# SEVENTEEN

The soft bed should have been comfortable, but it wasn't. Sage let her head sink into the pillow as she stared at the ceiling, thinking about Mason's ridiculous idea. No matter how hard she tried, she couldn't relax.

She didn't know him, not really. If she played her cards wrong, she could upset him and who knew how he'd react? The last thing she wanted to do was push him away and send him into rogue status. And knowing that living without a clan could turn a True into a Fallen, it was even more dangerous to let him go unchecked.

Sighing, Sage rolled off her bed and shuffled to her window. She pulled the drapes across and looked out to the boy's dorms. When they were practicing the shift, Mason had told her which room was his, so she counted the windows of the boys' second floor to find it. The lights were out.

A small flutter buzzed in her chest. She pressed her face to the window, reaching to see his bike in the parking lot. There was Mason, leaning against it. His legs were crossed at his ankles, the top one shaking.

He glanced at his watch.

Sage pulled her phone out to check the time. Nine forty. By the time she looked back, Mason was on his bike.

"Stupid boy," she muttered, watching him drive off.

As soon as the bike turned the corner, Sage's heart lurched. It fell to her stomach and sat there fizzing away. Every second that passed brought a deeper pang with it.

"Dammit!" Sage yelled, grabbing her jacket.

There was no time to creep through the corridor or worry about who could have been watching her. Sage tore through the girls' dorm and burst out into the cold night air. She'd barely hit the tree line when she shifted. It didn't take long to catch up to him. She flew in front of his bike at the intersection, where the long school driveway met the road to Burrville.

Mason screeched his bike to a halt, tire marks blackening the bitumen behind him. He lifted his helmet, displaying an irritating grin. "Couldn't stay away from me, huh?"

"Yeah, yeah," Sage said, unhooking the spare helmet from the back of the bike. "That's exactly it."

Her tone reeked of sarcasm, but the words were truth. That nagging tug in the pit of her stomach warned her not to leave him alone. Being a Guardian on call sucked.

The old brewery was all but abandoned. Black mold splayed from the roof like wet paint, wooden slates were cracking, and cobwebs lined all the boarded up windows. The only thing that gave away some kind of occupancy, were a few cars parked along the road.

Mason led her around the back of the building to a basement entrance. He creaked the door open, revealing a dark downward staircase. Sage followed him down, her hand reaching for his back.

She didn't touch him, she would never do that. It was only in case, you know, a Fallen appeared and she needed to protect him.

Mason glanced over his shoulder. "Are you okay?"

"We shouldn't be here," she warned.

A hint of concern flashed across Mason's face. It didn't last long. He blew a raspberry and waved his hand dismissively. "It'll be fine."

A closed door waited at the bottom of the stairs. Mason wrapped his fingers around an out-of-place, shiny, bronze handle and pushed the door open.

They walked into a small and crowded space. Wooden walls, like a rustic log cabin, lined the window-less room. Dim light shone from lamps that sat on walls and pendants that hung from the ceiling. Sage let out a small breath, relaxing a little. It was homey, in an earthy welcoming sort of way.

One lone snooker table hidden in a nook to the right was surrounded by loud burly men and a tall woman with tattoos covering both her arms. They laughed boisterously above the soft country music that wafted from a small speaker on the end of the bar. And on the left, a line of booths were occupied by an eclectic mix of people with many shapes and sizes and ethnicities.

A varnished tree trunk centered the room like a beam of light. It was circled by stools and a sweet wooden shelf. Beside it, three women in their early twenties danced without a care in the world.

The bar held the length between the snooker nook and the booths. It was manned by a bartender with long black hair, tanned skin, and "old soul" eyes. Sage stayed close to Mason as he strode across the room.

"We'd like a drink," Mason said, sounding way too much like a teenager.

The bartender raised his brows, shifting his gaze between the two students. "ID?"

Sage tugged on Mason's arm and whispered, "We

should just go."

He looked down at her with a bemused grin. Eyes flashing red he turned to face the bartender. As the bartender stared back at Mason, Sage felt her heart pace in cycles against her ribcage.

The bartender's bottom lip rolled out and he sniffed before turning to Sage. "And yours?"

Sage shot a look at Mason, shaking her head. The last thing she wanted was to spread her wings and draw attention. She gave him a silent plea, one that said, *This is trouble. We are definitely pushing the limits.* But Mason simply nodded in return, urging her to do what he just did.

She swallowed and turned shyly back to the bartender. Clutching the bar to steady herself, she called her owl forward and opened her eyes wide. As soon as the owl aligned with her and a flash of purple lit her eyes, she pushed it back again before her wings or talons could grow.

It was all the bartender needed. "What'll it be?"

"Bourbon," Mason said too quickly.

Sage winced. The only time she'd had a drink was when Camila smuggled rum into her room on her birthday. And that wasn't exactly her favorite taste. "Umm... margarita?"

Mason held in a laugh as he swung his head to her. "A margarita? Fancy pants."

Sage shrugged. Her aunty used to drink them all the time, it was the first thing she could think of. In a hurry to change the subject, Sage turned her back to the bar and scanned the room. "Brown hair, huh?"

The woman with the tattoos was out, she had short black hair. The dancing girls all had a variant of blond. And the few people in the booths who were brunette, didn't seem to have both long and wavy hair, let alone mood rings.

"Well, it could have been black or maybe auburn, hard to tell under these lights," Mason said, passing her the margarita. He motioned to a few stools at the end of the bar and began walking toward them.

Sage didn't know whether to laugh or cry. Mason was so care-free about, well, everything. If only life could be that simple.

"Great, well that narrows it down," Sage said to herself.

She rolled her eyes and took a quick sip of her drink. As the sweet fizzy tang bubbled down her throat, she danced a little inside. No wonder it was Aunt Blair's go-to drink. After taking another sip, she walked to Mason and climbed onto a bar stool.

"So," she said, placing her drink on the bar. "Where did it happen?"

Mason scooted his stool closer to hers and reached in front of her to point to the middle of the room where the wooden log reached to the ceiling. "See that beam there, I was leaning against the shelf, wondering what the heck I was doing here. I was trying to find someone who looked friendly enough to ask for a favor."

"A favor?" Sage turned to face him.

"Yeah, to talk to my brother and tell him that marking him was a no go."

Sage pinched the stem of her glass and twisted her fingers around it. "You really don't think he'd make a good Guardian, do you?"

"I don't know what I think," Mason said, as a woman with shoulder-length brown hair walked by. He followed her with his eyes. "He has a temper—"

"No kidding," Sage chided.

Mason snapped his attention back to Sage. "But he's not all bad. He apologized for the whole thing, you know?"

"You mean, killing you. That whole thing?" Sage felt anger rise within her. Mason's forgiveness was lost on her.

"Anyway," Mason said. "That's where the woman marked me. I saw her hand and the back of her head as she walked off."

Sage sighed, taking another look around the room. "She could be anyone."

"Yep," Mason said, sliding his fingertip over the rim of his glass. He grabbed his drink and took a large sip. Wincing, he stood. "You want to dance, don't you?"

"What? Why would I? No!"

A cheeky smirk appeared as Mason pointed to the ground. "You've been tapping your feet the whole time."

As Sage glanced down, Mason grabbed her wrist and dragged her to the middle of the room. He let her go and began to sidestep. His hair fell over his face as he swung his head in time with the boppy beat.

Sage would have laughed. She wanted to laugh. But he looked so damn hot. The way he smiled, teeth bared. The constant glint in his eyes, as though he knew the secret of life.

No matter what the hell that may have been going on in this godforsaken school, there was a light in him —a reckless abandon that Sage never had. It was in Camila, too. And her aunty.

She stood still, watching Mason and wondering how on earth she could find this *thing* she was missing.

"What's wrong?" Mason asked, clutched both her wrists. He began swinging her arms side-to-side. "Loosen up, Bright Eyes."

She didn't even flinch at the nickname her mother used to call her. Stepping closer to him, she asked. "Am I that uptight?"

His brows dropped, the swagger in his step coming to a standstill. He let his hand glide from her wrist to her hand and weaved his fingers through hers. With a voice softer than she ever thought he could use, he said, "No. Well...maybe just a little."

His proximity hastened her breath. Her eyes drifted to his lips, full and smiling. If he leaned any closer, she would let him kiss her.

*How reckless,* she thought to herself.

Surely, Mason couldn't call her uptight if she kissed him right there and then in the middle of a bar.

# EIGHTEEN

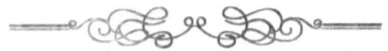

*Screw it!* Sage thought, deciding not to wait for him to make the first move.

She squeezed Mason's hands and pulled him closer. His exhale breezed over her face—the sensation sending her heart into overdrive. She watched his gaze dip to her mouth and back up to her eyes. Pulse racing, she tilted her chin upward and stared at his lips, wondering if they'd taste like bourbon.

"What are you doing?" Mason grinned, stepping back. "Do you want to kiss me?"

Embarrassed, she ripped her hands from his. A nervous laugh filled the air between them. "Pfff," she blurted. "Of course not."

All spark left his expression and a deep wrinkle formed between his brow. In that very moment, it occurred to her that maybe she really did need to loosen up. Sage held her finger up, then ran to the table where they left their drinks. She picked up her margarita with one hand and Mason's bourbon with the other. In quick succession, she sculled them both. As the bourbon burned her throat, she stuck her tongue out and glanced back at Mason. He stood where she left him with his hand over his mouth and a twinkle in his eyes.

Sage swiveled back to the bar and slapped her palm onto the mahogany. "I'll have another, please."

The bartender mixed her drink and placed it in front of her. She paid for it and held the stem between her fingers, taking a loud sip. A chuckle billowed beside her.

"What are you doing?" Mason asked.

Sage shimmied her shoulders. "Loosening up."

"Yeah?" Mason gently tapped on her glass. "Take it easy, though."

She slowly sipped her drink, keeping her eyes on him the whole time. As the buzz of alcohol soared through her blood stream, she let go. Of the fear. Of her past. Of everything. There was only her, him, and the music.

They danced, then. For lord knows how long. She let her arms swing around as her hips swayed in time with the music. The more they danced, the closer they became. Her palms found his chest, his hands rested on her hips. And soon, his touch made its way from her hips to her face, thumbs caressing her cheeks and his fingertips kneading the nape of her neck.

The sight of his hungry eyes warmed her chest and sent heat rushing through her veins. He re-grasped his hold on her neck and his fingers crossed over her leather necklace and its coarse latch. *Stay out of trouble.* His lips twitched as he leaned in and when his mouth was barely an inch away, Sage jerked back.

"Is it hot?" she flustered. "Are you hot?"

Okay, so maybe she couldn't loosen up completely.

"You want some water?" Mason asked.

Sage nodded.

Mason went to the bar, leaving her alone on the dance floor. She stepped side-to-side, cringing at how awkward she must have looked. She let her hands float above her as she moved, trying ever so hard to relax.

"Here you go," Mason said, holding out a tall glass of water.

Sage came to a halt. As she took the glass, something behind Mason caught her eyes. Wavy red hair—deeper than Arielle's, obviously dyed. The woman who wore it was around twenty years old, or so Sage guessed.

She was pretty but had a stern look on her face and seemed to be in deep conversation with someone. Sipping the water, Sage studied the woman. Intrigued, she peered around Mason to see who she was talking to.

There, sitting in the booth opposite this beautiful woman was another Guardian, someone Sage knew. Makoto. He didn't look happy—arms flailing and mouth moving sharply with each word he spoke.

"Shit!" Sage shoved the glass back into Mason's hands. "We gotta go!"

"Why?" Mason put the glass on the bar and turned to see what she had spotted.

Before he could get a glimpse, Sage grabbed his hand. She positioned his body between her and Makoto's sight, and rushed them toward the door. If she was drunk before, she was sure as hell sober now.

As they broke ground level and clambered outside, Mason began laughing. "What's gotten into you?"

"It isn't funny," Sage huffed, heading for Mason's bike. "None of this is funny. Makoto was in there. Can you imagine what would have happened if he saw us?"

"He was?" Mason asked, following her. "Well maybe we should go back? We could ask him—"

"No. Just no," Sage interrupted. She fumbled with the latch that attached the spare helmet to the bike. No matter how hard she pulled, it just wouldn't click open.

Sage gave up on the helmet, throwing her arms in the air. She let the bubbling frustration simmer to the surface and as she let out a wild roar, she half shifted. Talons reached from her nails and she felt her back twinge, ready to grow wings.

Mason reached around her and while keeping his

curious eyes on her, he set the helmet free with a simple squeeze. He held it out for her. "Be careful, your purple is glowing."

Sage glared at him, wings unfurling behind her. Not too far away, thunder cracked across the sky. "Aren't you ever serious?" she growled. "Don't you see how important it is to me?"

"To have an untarnished record? Yeah, I get it. Everything has to be perfect for you." He waved the helmet for her to take. Tiny droplets of rain fell onto the round surface.

Sage stared at the offering, taking in his words. But they didn't sit well within her, they couldn't be true. She was far from perfect. That position was given to Nadya. "I don't want to be perfect."

"Ha!" Mason guffawed, raising his brows in disbelief. "Could have fooled me."

"Yeah?" Sage snapped. "Well, it's better than being a reckless immature jerk who doesn't care what his actions do to him or anyone else."

Mason's demeanor dropped along with his shoulders. "Ouch."

His expression gave her guilt. She didn't want to upset him, but she didn't quite feel like herself, like something important had displaced within. As if she was changed... as if *he* had changed her.

The skies opened above them and proper rain pelted around them. Sage flinched as droplets streamed over her styled hair. She snatched the helmet and turned it around in her hands. Then, she jerked her arm around and threw it into the forest. It smacked through branches and crashed somewhere thirty odd yards away. Turning around, she panted, "How's that for perfect?"

Mason didn't reply. Instead, his head tilted to the side, eyes widening. Sage heard it, too. The door to the bar had opened.

Without a moment's hesitation, they bolted past the bike, across the wet road and into the darkened forest. About five trees in, Sage slowed. Hidden behind a tree, she peered through dense branches, watching Makoto and his red-haired friend get into a car.

Her knees wobbled beneath her as she stared with her owl's purple eyes, waiting for Makoto to drive off. Still half-shifted, too on edge to be anything else, she crouched low and let her knees connect to the woodland floor. As the car passed, she let her head fall to her knees.

When the sound of the engine had all but disappeared, Mason knelt beside her. "I found the helmet."

Sage peeped through the strands of her hair. Mason held his helmet, crushed on one side. She muttered, "Sorry. That's what happens when I lose control."

"You can't control everything, you know?"

"I just want to graduate," she said, tears stinging her eyes. "But what I did to you... that... that's unforgivable."

Mason shook his head. He clutched the helmet and stood. A growl emanated in the back of his throat and Sage watched him as he re-gripped the helmet, bringing his arm back. He thrust his arm forward and, like Sage had done earlier, he let the helmet go. It soared through the air, breaking the clearing and skidding along the old brewery's roof.

He spun to face Sage, eyes burning red. As he grimaced, fangs popped between his lips. "What if it wasn't your fault?"

"Well." Sage dug a talon into the tree trunk beside her and pulled herself up. "It wasn't my fault, it was your brother's."

"Exactly," Mason said. "If you didn't turn me I would have died. Won't Makoto understand that?"

Sage yanked her talon from the wood and stared at it. "Maybe"

Mason nodded and returned to human form. "Okay. It's something, right?"

Sage shook her head. She wasn't ready to be optimistic. She'd seen firsthand how quickly things could spiral out of control.

"What do you need? How can I help you?" Mason asked, earnestly.

"Turn back time? Go back to the night you first came to this stupid bar and don't go in. Tell your brother to get over the fact he won't be a Guardian."

Mason's face dropped. The sight of his shocked eyes made her heart sink, but now that she'd started, there was no turning back. "If you can't do that and you still get marked, don't try and get my attention to help you. And if you can't do that, then at least just ask me for help first. Don't force me to follow you. And if you can't do that, then don't let your brother hurt you. Kill him first."

"Stop!" Mason moved closer, chest rising and crashing with every heavy breath. "You don't know the truth."

Somehow, she'd always known there was more. There was something he'd held back.

"Then tell me," she pleaded.

Mason winced and the shadows above him cast an unnerving shadow around his glowing eyes. He reached for Sage and took her hand. They were silent as he led her deeper into the forest. After a few minutes, a small clearing appeared, and he let her hand go to sit on a fallen log.

Out from the canopy of branches, rain still fell. Sage didn't care—she stepped into the clearing, letting the coolness seep over her, and waited for him to speak. But he just sat there on the soaked log, staring into the nothingness around them. Without warning, he stood and walked around the log to face Sage. He gazed at her for a moment, strands of hair sticking to his forehead, before spinning on his heels and pacing back to the other side of the log.

Sage leapt over the log and reached out to clutch his wrist. "Mason!" she commanded. "Tell me."

Mason swallowed and took a long breath in. Tears welled in his eyes as he said, "I knew."

"You knew what?" Sage frowned, searching his clouded eyes for answers.

"That he was going to kill me." Mason's voice shook. "It was the plan."

Sage dropped his hand. "What?"

Mason raked his hands through his damp hair, eyes lifting to the treetops. "He knew I'd been marked at the bar and I told him that I was going to try and get the society to help me remove it. But when you showed up at the boxing studio, he saw you sitting there on the roof. He told me it was best that I was turned by a True. But the only way to get around Makoto's rules was to make it impossible for you to refuse. So he—"

"You planned it?" Sage shrieked. Her heart turned itself into knots. "You purposefully ruined my life?"

"No!" Mason raised his hands in surrender. "No, Sage, please. I didn't agree to it. I didn't want him to. Remember? I didn't want this! That was the truth. And when I was arguing with him in the alley, that was real. I didn't want to force you to do it."

Sage so desperately wanted to believe him. She wanted him to be a good guy. As she watched a tear roll down his cheek and meet with a raindrop, she realized why this made her heart ache. She liked him. Once she allowed herself to feel it, she couldn't take it back. Not now that she finally admitted it to herself. She liked him. She *really* liked him.

"You ruined my life," she whispered, letting her own tears fall.

Mason's eyebrows fell. He didn't reply, only nodded. As he wiped his cheek with his palm, he stepped closer.

Sage felt like screaming, like punching, like fully shifting and flying away. As he stepped closer, she balled her fist. Everything within her told her that he was trouble.

The truth was, despite her raging insides, she didn't think he'd ruined her life. If she hadn't turned him, she wouldn't know him. He was annoying and cocky and reckless and defied everything she believed in. But he also pushed her out of her comfort zone and that was thrilling. She'd found things in herself she never knew she wanted. With him she felt alive.

He moved in, so close their toes almost touched. He reached for her, hand hovering an inch from her shoulder. Barely whispering, he asked, "Is this okay?"

Sage had no words, but his hand cupped her shoulder anyway. Gently at first, and the longer she let him stay, the tighter his grasp became. It almost felt like he was loosening the constraints she'd built around her heart. Sage held her hands up to her chest, as if protecting herself. It was then that Mason pulled her to him, embracing her fully.

She had no fight left, if it was even there to begin with. Sage let her head fall onto the dip between his neck and shoulder. Elbows bent inward, she twisted her hands to his biceps. The ache inside her chest overflowed and she let it cascade out of her, sobbing without shame.

As the rain fell around them, for what felt like an eternity, she didn't break away. She let him hold her. And it felt like home.

# NINETEEN

It was almost midnight when they returned to campus. Mason took the school driveway and Sage flew through the forest to the top of the dorms. They had planned to go to their respective rooms and reconvene the next afternoon, but somehow Sage hovered at the forest edge, unable to let go of the night.

She shifted back to human form and sat, not caring about the damp grass beneath her. Purple hair hung in strands around her face, still dripping from the earlier downpour. It was cleansing, in a way. At the same moment that she finally succumbed to her emotions, the heavens opened up, as if applauding her courage.

Mason parked his bike near the boys' dorm and glanced up to where she sat. He was still for a moment and she wondered if he could see her in the shadows. Then, his eyes flashed red and she knew that he could.

Her heart flipped as he began walking up the hill toward her. She straightened her matted hair, as though she didn't just say goodbye looking the same way. He strode confidently, without a care in the world —something that would have annoyed her a day earlier.

"You know," Mason said as he reached her. "I've been thinking..."

Sage kept a straight face as she teased, "I hope it wasn't too difficult."

"Ahh." Mason grinned and pointed at her. "Now, who's the jester? Can we talk properly for one minute, Sage? Honestly."

Sage tried not to smile. This guy, he was nothing like she thought he was. Irritating, yes, but also endearing. She watched him as he dropped beside her and casually hung his elbows over his knees. She said, "Tell me, what have you been thinking?"

"Well, I know you said that I'll teach you boxing and you'll teach me how to shift and then we go our separate ways... but, I, ahh..." He scratched at his neck, his gaze firmly on Sage. "I was wondering if you'd reconsider? The going separate ways part."

Sage chortled. "I thought that was obvious."

"Good!" Mason sat up straight, letting his arms fall behind him. He leaned back onto his elbows. "I kinda assumed you'd never want to see me again. Especially after knowing the truth about Ben's plan to get you to turn me."

"Yes, well. It's *him* I have a problem with, not you."

Mason glanced at Sage, eyes filled with the warmth of a fireplace at Christmas. He gazed at her for a moment before his eyes twitched and his mouth lifted into a smirk. There was a distinct mocking tone in his voice as he said, "You're not going to kill him, are you?"

"Why not? I've broken two rules, why not three?" Sage was joking but thinking of Ben's sick plan to make sure she turned Mason swiftly changed her mood. "I honestly don't know why you're even talking to him after he did something so vile to you."

"He's my blood..." Mason paused before adding, "And I love him."

Sage frowned. She knew that blood didn't mean

much. "He stole your right to choose. That doesn't sound like love to me."

Mason sat up again, jaw clenching. "He would never have done that if he didn't know you'd turn me to save me."

The fact that Mason couldn't see that his own brother didn't care about him infuriated her. If he was that blind to it, Sage didn't think that anything she said would make a difference, but she said it anyway, "How would he know for sure I'd turn you? Seems to me like he gambled with your life."

Mason tried to smile, but his lips curved down. Sliding fingers over a blade of grass, Mason said, "He dreamed of being a Guardian his whole life. You know, if he didn't have such a temper, he'd probably be following right now in our father's footsteps. But the truth is, dad got sick of his constant manipulations in trying to be marked. He hasn't been welcome home for three years. He's only trying to be let back into the fold."

Sage was beyond holding her tongue. She liked Mason, which made the whole situation worse. Seeing him being used by his brother broke her heart. "You're making excuses for him. Whether confident that you would be saved or not, the fact is, your brother killed you. There is no excuse for that, not in my world."

Mason winced as though her words struck a chord. "It was all he had and now *I'm* all he has. He was told he would never become a Guardian. I don't want to dismiss him, too. Can you imagine that? Having family reject you because you weren't enough for them?"

A lump formed in Sage's throat. She'd lived through that. "Yes," she snapped, "I know."

"You do?" Mason looked shocked.

Sage couldn't bear to look him in the eyes. The thought of reliving her childhood was enough to make her want to hurl. But she knew that Mason needed it. Swallowing hard so the tears wouldn't rise, she pulled the ties from her braids and weaving her fingers through her wet hair.

With her hands busy, she tried to sound nonchalant as she explained, "My aunty. She took me in after my parents died. She hated it. I could tell. I was eight and apparently such a burden on her."

Sage stopped for a moment to pull a scrunchie from her wrist. She darted her eyes to Mason and tied the ends of her hair. Purple locks fell out of the loose hold. Dropping her hands to her lap, she continued, "My aunty would tell me almost every day how different her life would've been without having to take care of me. I get it, she'd lost her sister and looked at me as though it was all my fault. So, not only did I lose both my parents, I lost an aunty, too."

Sage swallowed, almost relieved at the splurge. Inhaling deeply she turned her torso toward him. "Don't you get it? The fact that she's my blood, doesn't mean I owe her. Just like you don't owe your brother."

When she finally looked at Mason, she found him staring at her, mouth agape. "I didn't know," he said. "Your parents died?"

"That's not the topic," Sage said quickly, regretting the choice to bare her soul. "The thing is, you need to stop defending your brother."

Mason rose, locking his fingers and wrapping them at the back of his neck. He looked out to the school field and sighed. "I can't just give up on him because he did one selfish thing."

So close. Sage knew she was getting to him. She hated saying the words, but he needed to hear them. "Ugh, he's using you, Mason. You would have died. Can you let that sink in, just for one moment can you hear me? He killed you."

"Stop," Mason yelled to the night sky. His voice rolled down the hill and echoed through the campus.

Sage leapt to her feet and grabbed his shoulders, forcing him to turn around and look her in the eyes. "Listen, I get it. My aunty fed me, clothed me, gave me soup when I was sick. But does that make it right that she left for a whole weekend when I was eleven and let me fend for myself? Or that she drank herself to oblivion the first four months of me living with her? Or that she sent me to this school at the first chance she could so she could finally travel the world without responsibilities? We don't owe these people anything. We walk away from them, vowing to never treat anyone else the way they've treated us."

Mason was silent for a while. As his eyes flitted between hers, they softened. With a small smile, he said, "You're amazing. You know that?"

"Yeah? Well you are, too." Sage pressed a pointed finger against his chest. "If only you had people around you who didn't treat you like crap."

He stepped closer and reached for her face, tucking a stray hair behind her ear. "I think I already do."

The touch was like a switch. Sage felt her blood heat and pool at her cheeks. She averted her gaze. "I've never told anyone much about my aunty. I mean they know dribs and drabs but—"

"It's safe with me. You're safe with me. I won't hold it against you..." Mason let his hand relax around the bottom of her ear, his thumb caressing her cheekbone.

Her body reacted—heart skipping a beat, warmth moving from her cheeks to other places. Sage lifted her face. This guy was too much.

"If," he said, grimacing a smile. "You maybe promise to drop the whole brother thing?"

Sage exhaled loudly as she studied his expression, full of hope. She guessed that if Mason was okay with it, then that was something he'd need to live with. She'd just have to forget about it, at least for the time being.

"I can do that," she whispered.

"Thank you," Mason replied, lifting his other hand to cradle her face. He added, "Floss."

Sage wanted to roll her eyes, but she couldn't keep them off him. His tensed jaw. His earnest gaze. His quickening breath.

A flash of light near the girls' dorm caught Sage's attention. On high alert, she tore herself away. As she squinted, trying to focus in the moonlight, Mason's hand hovered in the air for a moment before he let it fall.

"Sage?" he whispered.

At the forest end of the girls' dormitory, two sapphire-like eyes searched the perimeter. They blinked, then vanished. There were only two Guardians with an aura that color. Caspar and Nadya.

"Sit down." Sage blurted, pushing Mason down. She couldn't risk Mason's tiger being seen. If Nadya or Caspar looked at him while half-shifted, they'd see he was a Guardian.

Sage stood over Mason, her mind racing.

That was what loosening up did. It made her forget about what was important. It made her exposed. It made trouble.

"Is everything okay?" Mason asked.

"I should go," she said, backing up.

Mason lurched forward, "Will I see you tomorrow?"

Sage half-shifted to give herself strength. She pushed against his chest, forcing him back down. Returning to human form, she scolded, "I said sit. Stay here. We can't be seen on campus. Not out in the open. The arrangements of our deal don't change."

Even in the cloud covered moonlight, she still saw the heartbreak in his eyes.

It was necessary, she decided. It was better to break his heart than to risk her secret being revealed. But looking at him made her question everything.

A surge of fear and excitement buzzed through her veins. He was cracking her open, or rather, showing her how to fill in all the missing pieces. And she wanted more. More excitement. More life. More of him.

In that moment, she couldn't quite remember why the secret was so bad.

And, so she wouldn't change her mind, she leaned

over him, took his jaw with one hand, and planted her lips square on his.

He didn't taste like bourbon as she first thought. He tasted like morning walks and misty rain and evergreen leaves. Like that time between winter and spring. He tasted like life renewed.

Pulling away, she gasped, "But yes, I will see you tomorrow."

# TWENTY

Sage felt as light as air. She walked along the cobblestone path, swinging her arms and smiling—actually smiling. Well aware of her mood but not caring one bit who noticed, she entered the academic building, holding her head high. As she flung her locker open and grabbed her math book, she felt her phone buzz inside her blazer pocket.

A text from Mason lit up the screen. *Can I see you? Courtyard. Now.*

Sage's smile grew. It was against their agreement to be seen together on campus, but she wasn't in the least bit surprised that he didn't care. And if she was honest with herself, the whole thing was getting less worrying and more exciting.

Camila rested an elbow against a locker and leaned toward Sage. "Where the heck did you go last night?"

Sage bit into her bottom lip to reduce her grin. Faking ignorance, she said, "Huh?"

Frowning, Camila's eyes dropped to the phone in Sage's hand. She snatched the phone. "Oooh, how romantic. A lovers' meeting."

"It's not like that," Sage said, whipping the phone

out of Camila's grasp and locking the screen.

"You have got to be kidding me!" Camila dropped her head and looked at Sage as if she were peering over invisible glasses. "You and I are best friends, right? You think I can't see that weird glimmer in your eyes. Something happened. Holy crap, what's happened?"

Sage grimaced. "Nothing?"

"Ha!" Camila guffawed, smiling. "Liar."

Sage returned the smile and closed her locker. She cleared her throat and brushed past her best friend.

"Just like that, huh?" Camila called after her. "Is that all you're gonna give me?

Spinning around and walking backward, Sage said, "I'll see you in class."

One quick wave later, Sage kicked up her heels. Running wasn't allowed in the corridors, but she had almost hit a full sprint by the time she reached the courtyard. She burst through the doors and spotted Mason sitting on a table, toes balancing on the edge of a seat.

The sight of him made her heart flutter. His head was low, sending brown tendrils of hair over his brows. Shoulders curved in such a way that made his muscles bulge. He rested his elbows on his bouncing knees.

He looked nervous. Did she make him nervous? A rush of anticipation surged through her.

When the door shut behind her, Mason swung his head around. Sage half expected to see that innocuous grin of his, but instead there was only sadness in his eyes.

Noticing her, he pushed his hands against his knees. "Hi. There's something I have to tell you."

He said the words quick, as though he was pulling off a Band-Aid.

"What?" Sage asked, walking over.

As she approached, he turned away from her and hung his head, smothering his face with his hands.

She ran the rest of the way and smoothed her hand across his back. "What is it?"

"Sage?" A curt voice came from the other side of the courtyard.

Sage glanced over her shoulder to find Nadya looking at them. Her eyes bounced between the two of them for a moment before settling on Sage. "Can I talk to you?"

Sage made her way around the tables, annoyed at the intrusion. Nadya probably wanted to make some remark about her being tardy. *Always with the backhanded comments to make me feel less than perfect.*

Before Sage even reached her, Nadya said, "I'm just gonna spit this out. What were you doing last night?"

It was uncharacteristic for Nadya to blurt or seem unconsidered with her speech, and there was a twinge of urgency in her tone. Sage felt the color leave her face. "Last night?" she said, forcing herself not to look at Mason. She shrugged and offered, "Sleeping?"

Nadya's steely expression didn't change. "No, you weren't. Not until after midnight."

Sage swallowed, remembering the pair of beady blue eyes searching in the dark. She felt like she was being tested. But she couldn't cave in now, not after everything. Staring deep into Nadya's icy glare, she held her ground. "You seem to already know the answer. Tell me, what was I doing?"

"I saw you get on a bike. With him." Nadya peered over Sage's shoulder and pointed. "Then later, I saw you on the hill."

Sage nodded. Pursing her lips together, she waited for the follow up. The part where Nadya said she knew Mason was a Guardian and that Sage had turned him.

Still looking behind Sage, Nadya said, "Isn't that Mason?"

"Y... yes," Sage stammered.

"The bully from the library?" Nadya turned her

attention back to Sage, top lip curling. "A name on AJ's list?"

Nadya's fists clenched beside her, an unfamiliar expression casting over her face. Sage thought she looked as though she was about to break a rule and shift in public.

Putting her hands up in surrender, Sage whispered, "He's not a Guardian. Remember? I told you yesterday. It's just a coincidence."

Again, Sage waited for the onslaught—for Nadya to point her finger and say; *"I got you. I already know what you've been hiding."* But it never came. Nadya kept staring at Mason, and eventually said, "Are you sure?"

In that moment, all Sage could think about was that there was a chance, albeit a small one, that even in her half-shifted phase, Nadya still didn't see Mason's Guardian on the hill. So, she took that chance and ran with it.

"We snuck out."

Nadya's expression turned from rage to confusion. "Huh?"

"Last night. We snuck out to... to kiss." Sage said it loud enough that her truthful words echoed across the courtyard.

A chuckle from Mason bellowed behind them. And soon after, he stood beside her and swung an arm around her shoulders. "Yes. We are lovers. Isn't she amazing?"

"You're..." Nadya's eyes widened. "Together?"

It was a stupid confession, but it was better than the alternative. Sage took Mason's hand in hers, deciding to throw Nadya off the scent completely. "Yes."

"And that's how you know he's not..." Nadya smacked her lips together and finished her sentences with a nod.

"Right. That's how I know." Sage pulled her hand from Mason's and led Nadya to the door. She whispered, "Listen, I want to keep this a secret. It's been so awkward that he was involved in that whole library assignment thing. I don't want him to get caught in any of this." Sage glanced over her shoulder at Mason. He gave an awful cheesy grin and blew her a kiss. Rolling her eyes, Sage turned back to Nadya. "He's a soft gooey teddy bear on the inside and the whole Shadow Society truth will freak him the hell out."

Nadya crossed her arms. "Mmm, is that so? How come you didn't say anything before?"

Sage shrugged. "Embarrassed, I guess. You all think he's a bully."

Squinting, Nadya gave one last glare at Mason. She faced Sage, huffed, and went inside.

Sage's sigh emptied her lungs. She wandered back to Mason. "I can't tell if she believes me."

Mason placed his hand on her shoulder. "Don't look but she's watching us through the door."

As Sage moved to look, Mason clutched her jaw in his hands and turned her to him. She was greeted with something she'd never seen before. His face was sullen, sadness oozing from his eyes to his rolled out bottom lip.

"Pretend you're still into me," he whispered before moving his mouth toward hers.

Their lips locked and he threaded his fingers up and through her hair. He was polite, keeping his mouth closed. But Sage didn't need to pretend, and in a moment of weakness she clutched at his blazer and pulled him in closer, pressing her lips harder against his. The movement caused him to stir, a groan rumbled in the back of his throat. He opened his mouth then, caressing her lips in fluid motion.

As they parted, Mason's eyes danced between hers as if he was searching for something. His breath was heavy. He let his warm hands drop, leaving her cheeks to the cool air.

Sage tore her eyes from him to see if Nadya was

still watching, but she was gone. Turning back, she gave a cheeky grin and playfully punched his chest. "Why would I need to pretend?"

Mason stepped backward until his thighs hit a table. He clasped his hands together—fingers kneading knuckles. With a low voice, he said, "I need to talk to you."

"What's wrong?"

"I don't know how to say it. You'll be upset and I don't want you to be upset with me." His eyes drifted to the ground and he scuffed a heel onto the pavement. "I never intended to... get so involved with you."

Silence. Disbelief. A butterfly let itself loose inside her chest.

She could barely get the words out. "What are you saying?"

She knew what he was saying though. He regretted how close they had become. He regretted kissing her. Just when he'd helped her let go.

"Ben is in incubation, by the rate of his symptoms the mark will appear tomorrow or the next day." He said it so matter-of-factly, as though he was reciting a recipe.

Sage wasn't sure she heard right. "What?"

"He's been marked."

Heart rate rising, Sage relived the moment she decided to turn Mason. She felt the way her heart broke at the thought of this boy being beaten to death by his own cowardly brother. She saw the mortal blood that spilled from his lips. How time seemed to cease when he stopped breathing. But it was all a manipulation. She had been used by both of them.

They wanted to become Guardians at all costs, no matter who they brought down along the way. Of course Mason would mark his brother. She was an idiot for thinking otherwise.

The betrayal felt sour, like over ripe apples being forced down her throat. Sage didn't want to cry, but tears stung her eyes. She didn't want to ask why—she didn't want to know.

She stepped away from him.

Mason pushed himself off the table and rushed to her. "I'm so sorry. You have to understand that I never meant to hurt you or use you, but I know I've done both those things."

She turned her face to him, but her gaze couldn't quite reach his eyes. "Don't talk to me ever again."

Her heart broke as she tore herself away. She ran. From him—and the way he made her feel. Like an unwanted thirteen-year-old.

"Sage? You don't mean it!" he called.

She ignored him and the reflection of his lying face in the glass door.

He called for her again. "Sage, please?"

She opened the door and stepped inside. And as she slammed the door shut, she heard a whimper.

"Floss?"

But even that sorry excuse for a nickname couldn't make her stay.

# TWENTY ONE

Sage had already missed half her class. She wondered if there was any point in showing up for the rest. The Shadow Society lesson didn't start until second period, which meant Makoto was free. She charged through the faculty wing, scanning the doors for his name.

It wasn't until she tapped on his door that she realized what was about to happen. He was either going to kill her or kick her out of the society. No big deal.

As footsteps echoed inside Makoto's office, Sage grimaced and took a lung full of air. This was it. She was going to tell Makoto everything. The door creaked opened and a woman peered into the small gap.

"Hello?" The woman asked.

She had brown eyes and flaming red hair. Sage froze. It was the same woman she saw with Makoto at the bar the night before.

Sage waited for recognition to hit, but the woman just stared, holding the door half in front of her face. "Can I help you?"

Sighing, Sage almost laughed at herself. She was worried the woman had seen her at the bar. But it didn't matter, not any more. Not now she was going to tell Makoto everything anyway.

"Hi," Sage said, trying to get a glimpse into the office. "I'm looking for Makoto?"

"He's... not... here..." the woman replied, squinting. "Do you want him... for any... *particular* reason?"

Sage realized the woman was being cautious. She was asking something specific. Sage knew the answer. "I'm in the Shadow Society."

The woman sighed and opened the door fully. "Come in, I'm Tessa. I'll be taking your classes today."

Sage stepped into Makoto's office and Tessa shut the door. She pointed to an empty seat and took another one behind the desk. Sitting down, Sage asked, "Where's Makoto?"

"He's got his own assignment, so he called me to help you guys out until he's back." Tessa rested her elbows on the desk and leaned forward. "I'm an alumnus, so I know exactly what you're going through."

Sage gave a soft smile and chewed on the inside of her mouth. There was no way she could tell Tessa about her problems. *As if* she knew exactly what she was going through. Sage bet Tessa never turned anyone before graduation.

"Is everything all right?" Tessa asked.

Sage sat up straight. "When will Makoto be back?"

"I'm not sure. Assignments can take anywhere between a few minutes and a few years..." Tessa's voice petered out, her eyes drifting to the back wall. She snapped them back to Sage and smiled. "But don't worry, he's fast. Whenever he left during my year in the society, he'd be back the same day or the day after."

"Oh, okay." A day wasn't so bad. She could wait one day to tell him her mistakes.

"Is there anything *I* can help you with?"

The caring question sent an unexpected shock wave of emotion through Sage. As the warmth of tears teased her eyes, she wanted to ask Tessa if she or anyone she knew had ever misread their own gut instincts. But she thought better of it and asked, "How do you know that assignments are assignments?"

"Sometimes they are given to us by the Elders of the Veil, the ancient creatures who created Guardians. Have you learned about them yet?" Without waiting for an answer, Tessa continued, "Sometimes they just come to us."

Sage leaned forward. "What does that feel like?"

Tessa tightened her fists and hovered them in front of her stomach. "It's a feeling but also physical. It actually draws you where you need to go."

Sage remembered the almost magnet-like moments when she followed Mason, not once but three times. "Is that feeling ever wrong?"

Tessa shook her head and her beach curls bounced off her chin. "Never." She whipped her finger out and pointed at Sage. "And when you get that feeling you have to act quick. Those ones are the best ones and most important."

"Right." Sage scratched her neck and glanced around Makoto's room.

A collection of watercolor artworks lined a wall. All abstract—all shades of black and white and gray. He had a taste. Dark taste. A shiver ran down her spine.

Tessa inched to the edge of her seat and asked, "Have you had that feeling?"

Sage scrunched her nose and looked back at the new teacher. Through a nervous laugh she managed to say, "Nah."

Camila was waiting for Sage outside the Shadow Society lecture room. As soon as Sage approached, Camila threw her arms up. "Where the hell have you been? You didn't make it to class. What's going on with Mason? Are you sleeping together? Oh my god, I feel so left out."

Sage swung her arm over Camila shoulders and urged her inside the room. She whispered, "There's been a hiccup. Mason created this whole situation with his brother so I would turn him."

Camila pulled herself out from Sage's hold. Her mouth dropped open as her eyes widened, drifting to the space beside Sage's head. Her breath quickened, as though the room itself had earth's last air. She finally said, "How is that possible?"

"I don't know." Sage whipped her head to the door as Caspar and Arielle entered. She turned back to Camila, "I don't know what to do. Tell me what to do."

Swallowing, Camila shook her head. She clutched Sage's hand and dragged her to the middle row. As they dropped into their seats, Camila asked, "Do you think he's dangerous?"

The door clicked shut and Tessa walked in. She counted four heads. "Are we waiting on someone?"

"Sorry?" Arielle said, glancing back at Sage and Camila. "What do you mean?"

Tessa chuckled to herself and stood behind Makoto's desk. "My name is Tessa. Makoto is on assignment, so I'm your teacher until he gets back. There's usually five recruits."

"Oh, Nadya. She's uh." Caspar shifted in his seat. "She's looking after a sick friend."

"Sounds like a True Guardian," Tessa said, sifting through Makoto's drawer.

"Ugh," Camila whisper-moaned. "Nadya's her star pupil and she's never even met her."

Still sorting through the drawer, Tessa asked, "So, where are you up to in your lessons?"

Arielle cleared her throat and tucked her hair behind her ear. Smiling sweetly, she said, "Makoto just told us about the first Guardians."

"The first Guardians," Tessa repeated, lifting one piece of paper out of the pile. "Who's Sage?"

Sage felt her heart fall to her stomach. She slowly

raised her hand. "That would be me."

Tessa looked up. "Oh, that's you." She read the note again, then waved the piece of paper like a fan. "Makoto mentioned that you guys have an assignment. Any reports?"

"All good," Arielle blurted. "Pretty much done with."

Tessa sat down, half smiling. "Pretty much?"

"What she means is, done. It's done," Caspar lied.

Tessa brought the piece of paper to her lips, and like Makoto had done many times, she took her time eying each of the recruits in the room. She stared at Sage last, lingering a moment longer than the others. Then, she dropped the note inside the drawer and slammed it shut.

"Okay, animals." She pressed her palms against the desk and stood up. "Makoto may humor your bullshit but I'm not buying it. Someone better spill really soon, or I'm gonna wolf out on all your asses."

The four of them balked. There was no doubt Tessa meant business. The question was, who was going to buckle first?

In the front row, Arielle visibly shook, her eyes as wide as Sage had ever seen them. And that was saying something. Caspar kept a straight face, but his fingers strummed against his thighs. Tap. Tap. Tap.

"You know," Tessa said, moving around the desk. She leaned against it and crossed her ankles just like Makoto would. "I've seen some gnarly stuff. I've met a lot of Fallen." She gave a tiny lop-sided smirk and looked down at her fingers as the ends sprouted claws. She picked at them as though they were well-manicured nails.

"The one thing they all had in common was that they were faultless liars. They'd convince other wannabe Guardians of their innocence and turn them, creating an army of blood-thirsty monsters. Now, I know none of you would ever want to hurt a civilian, that's not what we train for. But sometimes..." Tessa lurched forward, her eyes a bright pink flare. Her voice rose. "Sometimes when you are deceived, innocents get hurt because of your carelessness and inability to notice."

Sage felt like Tessa was talking directly to her. Mason had deceived her and now he was a Guardian, and soon his brother would be, too. How many innocents will die because of her actions?

Beside Sage, Camila jolted, her butt lifting off the seat at least three inches. She clutched her chest and turned to Sage. "She scares the bejeebies out of me."

"Listen," Caspar said, rising. He held his hands out in defense. "It all just kind of got out of hand."

"Caspar, don't," Arielle pleaded.

Ignoring her, he continued, "Our assignment got marked and we don't know who did it. We've been afraid to tell Makoto."

Tessa's eyes returned to their normal brown hue. She nodded and slid her phone out of her back jean pocket. Shaking her head, she tapped the screen and held the phone to her ear. "Makoto? Yes. They spilled.... Took me five minutes..." Turning her back to everyone, she let out a few short cackles. "Umm, yeah, it's totally fine. Nothing we can't fix."

Caspar twisted around in his seat, looking back to his classmates. "What just happened?"

# TWENTY TWO

The Shadow Society recruits sat together at lunch time. Something they'd never done. Sage remained silent. With everyone's focus now on AJ and his mark, the urge to reveal her secret had dissipated.

Arielle shoveled the last of her chicken wrap into her mouth and stood. She muffled, "I'll go relieve Camila."

Caspar glanced at his watch. "She's only been with AJ for half an hour."

Cheeks puffing like a chipmunk's, Arielle shrugged and ran off.

"That's her third shift already," Caspar said, watching her leave.

Nadya gave a sad smile. "She feels like he's her responsibility."

Sage picked at part of her wrap, staring at the table where Mason told her what he'd done. Part of her wondered whether she'd see him again, or if now he'd gotten what he wanted he'd leave Graystone Academy. The other part of her scolded her for caring either way. She did, though. Care.

"Where's your boyfriend?"

Sage blinked a few times, snapping herself out of her daze. She moved her attention to Nadya, who was patiently waiting for an answer. A wry smile brightened her stern face.

"Her boyfriend?" Caspar asked, intrigued.

Nadya searched the courtyard. "There he is." She began waving manically to the back corner. "Come over!"

Sage spun in her seat. Sure enough, there was Mason, leaning against the back wall. She watched in horror as he sauntered over at Nadya's call.

"Him?" Caspar jeered. "Really?"

Mason slid in beside Sage, a wary smile on his face. "He-ey."

Forcing a smile back, Sage replied through gritted teeth, "Hi."

"What? No sickening embrace?" Nadya teased, clearly enjoying the scene. "You guys were all loved up this morning. Did you break up telepathically or something?"

"Nadya!" Caspar scolded.

Sage squeezed her eyes shut and she curled a finger underneath her leather necklace. She could almost imagine Nadya's face when she found out the truth. The golden girl shocked at Sage's recklessness. She considered coming clean, right there and then—

A gentle hand ran across her neck, fingertips kneading on her skin. Lips pressed against her temple. A warm exhale tickled her ear as Mason's deep raspy voice said, "Of course not."

Mason moved his hand from her neck to pinch her chin, he turned her face to him. Sage peeled her eyes open, one by one, her breath hitching at the closeness of him. His eyes hooded as he whispered, "Please don't give up on me."

Without thinking, she placed her palm directly onto his face—her fingers curving around his forehead —and pushed him back. "Don't embarrass me, Mason." She rolled her eyes at Nadya and Caspar. "He gets so P.D.A sometimes."

Mason wrapped his fingers around her wrist and

removed her hand from his face. He cleared his throat and said, "I can't help it. I mean, look at her. She looks like a goddamn angel sometimes."

Nadya's eyes turned to slits. "Sometimes?"

*Why did he have to say that?* Sage thought. He was insinuating he'd seen her wings... That she'd shown him her wings.

A shriek resonated behind them.

Someone, a cheerleader, burst past their table, tears lining her face. Her guttural and heart-wrenching moans echoed through the courtyard. Sage knew there was only one thing that could make someone cry like that. Grief.

The next table down erupted into a sea of uncontrollable sobs. Nadya rose to her feet, and with eyes square on the table, she marched over. As Nadya queried them, another cheerleader leapt from her seat.

As the girl rushed past, Sage jumped up, stopping her in her tracks. She clutched the girl's shaking shoulders. "What's happened?"

"Brian, Mal, and Ethan went missing last night. And..." her bottom lip quivered. "Mal was found this morning. He's dead."

Sage let her go. Mal was on the football team. They all were.

Nadya, shell-shocked, stood by the table of crying cheerleaders. Caspar scrambled to meet her. Sage looked for Mason, but he was already gone.

A tiny thought flashed through her mind. One that made her blood run cold. If Mason used her this whole time to get his brother to become a Guardian, what more was he capable of?

"We have to go." Caspar clicked his fingers in front of Sage's face. He grabbed Sage and Nadya by their wrists and headed inside, dragging them behind him.

"They said it was a bear or cougar." Nadya gasped as the three of them ran for the Shadow Society.

"Yep," Caspar puffed, charging ahead. "There's a Fallen loose on campus. And if we don't stop it soon, the worst is yet to come."

Sage's heart thumped hard beneath her rib cage. They were in over their heads. *She* was in over her head. Drowning before she even realized she was in too deep.

At the other end of the corridor, Camila steamed toward them. As they met outside the classroom door, she asked, "You heard?"

"Yes," the three of them echoed in unison.

Four hands smacked the door and they launched themselves in.

Tessa swiveled in Makoto's chair at the commotion. "Well, you guys are eager for class."

"We've got a problem," Caspar announced. "Well, *more* of a problem than we had before lunch anyway."

"Sit," Tessa commanded, standing up. She strode to the door and closed it. And when she turned back, she found the four recruits still standing. She repeated louder, "Sit."

Sage stepped back until her thighs hit a chair in the front row. She let herself fall into it. The tiny thought swirled in her mind like a record, volume growing louder. Her hands shook as she pushed the thought away. She couldn't go there, she couldn't think it. Surely, Mason wasn't capable of murder.

Beside her Camila muttered, "Is this really happening?"

"Okay," Tessa said, pacing in front of them. "Something has really shaken you all up. What's going on? Is AJ okay? Who's with him now, Arielle?"

Nadya was the only one of the four who remained standing. She extended her hand to Tessa. "Hi, I'm Nadya. All due respect but we don't know you. I'd prefer if we waited for Makoto."

Tessa curled her tongue around the corner of her mouth, giving a pithy smile as she studied Nadya. "Well, lucky for you he's already here. And no offense, Nadya, is it? You haven't experienced anything close to what I have. You're lucky to have me."

Nadya took a quick glance at Caspar, who nodded. She sniffed, cocked her chin, and sat down. "We'll wait for Makoto."

"That's fine by me. I've got an assignment in Cedar Falls anyway. Makoto just asked me to swing by on my way through. Because you bunch of ingrates don't know how to act like a clan. By this time in my training, we were living out of each others' pockets. We leaned on each other, we trusted each other. There were no secrets. We were a team, a family. You guys need to sort yourselves out, something isn't adding up and it needs to be dealt with before it's too late."

The door clicked and Makoto stepped in. His eyebrows rose, then dropped as he scanned the four of them sitting in the front row. He greeted Tessa with a hug. "You really did give them a stir up."

"Not enough," Tessa replied. She swung an arm down their line, like they were prizes on a game show. "There's something else they're hiding too. More than AJ being marked." She covered her mouth with her hand and whispered loud enough for them to hear. "They're scared."

Tessa walked toward the door without turning back. No goodbyes. Just a flippant wave as she left the room.

Makoto took Tessa's place, pacing in front of them. After his fifth walk by, he halted and swiveled on his heels. "So, AJ's been marked?"

"Yes sir," Caspar replied. "We've been on watch during his incubation. Arielle's with him now."

Makoto glanced to Sage . "Anything else?"

Sage opened her mouth, but only a squeak came out.

"It's bad." Camila leaned forward. "A boy was killed in the woods. Two others are missing."

Makoto flared his nostrils. "Right. That sounds serious. Is that all I need to know?"

His darkened eyes stared down at Sage as though waiting. As though he knew. That was her chance to get it out. To finally be rid of the burden.

She glanced away.

"It's a Fallen isn't it?" Caspar asked.

Makoto nodded. "Unless any of you broke my rules, then yes, we're dealing with a Fallen."

"Oh my god, this *is* happening." Camila ran her hands down her face, fear streaming out of her eyes. For all the times she wanted to face a Fallen, Camila's excitement was long gone. A ghost of her normal self.

It would have been funny to Sage—finally knowing that Camila was all talk—if she couldn't stop thinking about Mason.

The PA crackled and the Principal's voice boomed through. "Students. Due to our sudden and dreadful loss, all classes are called off for the afternoon. Please make your way to your dormitories in an orderly fashion while animal control surveys the campus. Stay vigilant and aware."

Makoto clapped his hands together. "Right, team. There's no lesson this afternoon. We have a new assignment and this time, I'm the lead. The whole school needs protecting. We need to find the Fallen who did these monstrous acts. We need to get their blood, cure AJ, and kill them. But we need to do it in secret. No matter how dire it gets, no civilian must know of our True existence. Is that understood?"

Everyone nodded.

"Go then!" Makoto snapped. "Caspar you're on boys' dorm, Nadya you are on girls'. Camila building A and Sage building B. I'm going to find the surveillance footage and scan it for anything. Report back here if anything changes."

Caspar and Nadya jerked to attention. Sage followed suit, helping Camila slowly rise to her feet. As they all marched behind Makoto, the thought rang like a megaphone through Sage's mind...

Mason was a Fallen.

And *she*—Sage Windsor, orphan and coward—had brought this hell to Graystone Academy.

# TWENTY THREE

Along with a plethora of panicked students, the Shadow Society scrambled down the corridor. Sage pushed her way past a crying Freshman to catch up with Caspar on his way to the boys' dorm. She bumped in beside him. "Caspar?"

"Yeah?" he asked, straining his head above the crowd.

"Can we swap?"

"Huh?"

"I need to protect the boys' dorms. Please..." she cringed at the words that came out of her mouth next. "Mason. My boyfriend. I need to make sure he's okay. Can you stay here in this building, please?"

Caspar slowed his pace and placed a hand on her shoulder. Nodding, he said, "Sure. Be careful."

"You too." She stepped toward him, an urge to give him a hug. But he turned around before she got the chance.

Sage took short, hasty breaths as she squeezed past

the swarm of boys heading for their rooms. She wasn't looking for a Fallen, she knew exactly where to go. When she found the right door, she pounded her fist against it.

Mason opened the door, a surprised look on his face. It was followed by a smile. "Sage? Oh my god, what the hell is—"

"Give me your blood," she demanded.

"What?" Mason frowned. "Why?"

Sage pushed him into his room and slammed the door behind her. For a split moment, she was distracted by her surroundings. A meticulously made bed, an Iron Man poster hanging on the wall, a bookshelf lined with history books and fiction, and a dark blue armchair sitting in front of the window. Her breath lengthened. It almost felt homey.

"Why do you need my blood?"

Shaking her head, Sage's heart rate rose. She pointed at him "Did you kill Mal?"

His mouth dropped open. "Why would I?" And then his jaw clenched. "You really think it was me?"

Sage started pacing. "I don't know. Makoto says that only certain types of people make good Guardians and the rest are at risk of becoming a Fallen. And you are..." She stopped pacing to look him up and down. "You're a little reckless already and—

"I'm not a Fallen." Mason took her shoulders. "I'm reckless, sure. But I'd never dream of killing anyone. I know how to use my strength. I'd never use it to hurt someone. And I have my dad, remember. I know what a True Guardian looks like."

Her head felt light. How could she know? How could she truly know? Makoto said that a Fallen great at deception. "You lie all the time."

"No, I don't." Mason sighed and let his hands drop to his side. "Not all the time."

"So, maybe you're not a True." Even as she said the words, her gut raged against them.

*Please say you are. Please say you are.*

Mason's fingers curled into fists. The edges of his jaw protruded. "I am."

He said what she wanted to hear but it didn't feel like enough. "So, why would you mark your brother even though I told you the rules?"

Mason laughed. He clasped his hands over his head and looked to the ceiling. "Oh, Floss." Returning his gaze to her, he said, "I didn't mark him. I never said that. I said he was marked. We don't know who by. Maybe by the crazed Fallen who marked me. Probably, most definitely by the same one who killed those jocks."

Sage's breath hitched. She stumbled until her back hit his door. "You didn't mark him?"

He closed the gap between them. With earnest eyes and warmth in his tone, he softly said, "No."

A weight lifted. She wasn't responsible for the death of Mal. And with Mason, she hadn't created a monster.

"Do you still need my blood?" Mason asked. Without waiting for her reply, he strode to his bookshelf and grabbed a small transparent container filled with paper clips.

She watched silently as he emptied the contents, half-shifted, and dug his claws into his palm. He dripped blood into the container and placed the lid carefully over it.

As he held the container out for her to take, Sage stared at the crimson droplets. Looking back to him, she pushed the container toward him. "I don't need it. I believe you."

"Take it anyway." Mason turned her hand around and placed it on her palm, curling her fingers around it. Still holding her hand, he leaned closer. "As a peace offering. As my apology."

"What are you sorry for?" she asked, placing it onto his bookshelf.

His lips lilted and a frustrating, yet endearing, glint lit his eyes. "That your white-haired friend likes me more than she likes you."

"Ugh." Sage rolled her eyes and pushed his chest. "I swear everything is a joke to you. Do you care about anything?"

Mason took a step. His eyes deepened. "I care about *you*."

Did he really mean it? Vulnerability swept through her. The leather against her skin felt like it tightened around her neck. Her mother's words rang through her head—*stay out of trouble.* Trouble, trouble, trouble.

Sage frowned at herself. Why were those the only words she recited? Her mom told her many things before her death. Things like "Take your shoes off, feel the grass between your toes," and, "Sage Windsor, how many times have I told you to believe in yourself? You can do more than you think."

But those weren't the last words she heard her mom say. The very last words told her to stay out of trouble. And, then days later, she was shipped off to live with her aunt, who loved her for a brief moment before wishing she never existed.

The words became a mantra for her to fall on when things felt out of her control. As if they were the only thing that would make everything okay in the end.

She remembered them at nine-years-old when Aunt Blaire told her to stay in her room or risk being grounded. She dared not leave that room for twelve hours straight, until her bladder felt like it was about to explode.

She remembered them at twelve-years-old when a school friend tried to get her to taste champagne at a sleep over.

She remembered them at sixteen-years-old when she joined the Shadow Society.

She remembered to stay out of trouble for years. Until Mason.

Dropping her head, Sage said, "Don't do that. Don't make light of all of this."

"I'm not making light. Look at me. Sage?" Mason

tucked his finger under her chin, forcing her to look up. "I'm being honest. I care about you. It's not a joke to me."

Why did he have to look at her like that? She wanted to be strong around him, but deep down she knew she was already a lost cause. There was no staying out of trouble with him.

"If I'm honest," Mason continued. "I'm not really this positive light-hearted guy. I mean, most of the time I'm this cool, but other times I revert to it because it's just how I cope with uncertainty. Sorry if that annoys you."

Sage shook her head. She wasn't annoyed, she was scared. Like the misleading comfort she felt when her aunty first took her in. "I just want to know if it's real."

Mason had inched so close that if she lifted her hand, she could rest it on his chest. If she leaned in, they could kiss.

She stared at his lips as he said, "You want to know what is real exactly? My personality or..." he winced.

A wave of bravery hit her and she rode with it. "I want to know if the way you look at me means something."

"It means something," he whispered, reaching for her.

He tucked her hair behind her ear. His eyes flitted between hers before they snapped to her lips. He kneaded his fingers into her skull, urging her closer still. As his breathe tickled her nose, she closed her eyes and waited for the sensation of his lips.

A loud cry resonated from the other side of the door. Footsteps stormed up and down the corridor. Mason tore away from Sage, and the sudden absence of his body close to hers left her cold.

"What the hell?" Mason said as he clutched the handle. He opened door carefully and peered through. A storm of boys ran in all directions.

Within a moment, a body came tumbling against the door, knocking it wide open. A freshman writhed on Mason's floor. His face was scratched, blood dripping from four places.

"What's going on?" Sage asked, bending down to inspect the wound. Even though she knew in her heart what it was. A Fallen, right there in the boys' dorm.

When she was satisfied the freshman was in no immediate danger, she jumped to her feet and joined Mason out in the corridor. Chaos swirled around them. Bodies lined the floor, some crying out, others lifeless. And right in the middle of it all was AJ—fangs protruding from his mouth, blood coating his lips and chin. Not longer the meek and nerdy student, muscles ripped at his T-shirt.

They were too late. He'd already been turned by a Fallen. The assignment was a failure. If she wasn't so hung up on Mason she would have been paying more attention to AJ. Protecting him. Maybe he wouldn't have even been marked.

As AJ stepped over a body and dug his claws into another's side, Mason roared. He'd already half-shifted, red eyes blazing like a smoke covered sun. He leapt for AJ, tearing him off the innocent boy. Sage bolted for the wounded body, pressing her hands against the deep bloody cuts.

She looked up in time to see Mason throw AJ. His head thumped against the wall and then he wilted to the ground. Mason stood over him, fist ready to give another blow.

In the other direction, Caspar and Nadya barreled down the hallway. Still running, Nadya noticed the boy under Sage's hold and grabbed her phone. As she dialed for an ambulance, Caspar diverted to Mason.

He balled his hand and pulled his arm back, ready for impact. Eyes burning neon blue he yelled, "Stop right there!"

"Wait!" Sage leapt to her feet. "He's not the bad guy. Look at AJ!"

On the floor, unconscious at Mason's feet, AJ lay limp. Blood dripped from his fangs, down his chin, and pooled on the floor. A spiral mark curved around his neck.

Caspar pointed at Mason as they both returned to human form. He shot his eyes to Sage and he said, "Was *this* your secret?"

# TWENTY FOUR

"I knew something was up with you!" Caspar said, pacing Mason's room. "We gave you the chance to tell us. We offered to help."

"She didn't want it," Nadya scoffed.

Camila let out a long and loud groan. "Chill out, guys. I'm sure he's good. If Sage believes in him, we believe in him. Like a clan should, right?"

On the floor at the end of Mason's bed, AJ stirred. He moaned, eyes twitching. Within a second, Caspar sent his fist against AJ's jaw, knocking him out again.

He turned to Mason. "And what do you say all about this?"

Mason sat next to Sage on his bed. He rested his elbows on his knees, not knowing who to look at. Five faces stared at him. Including Sage, who was desperately hoping he'd opt to say something profound instead of some lame quip.

He leaned toward her and whispered, "Does this mean I'm in the society?"

"I can't believe you turned someone," Arielle said, hands sifting through her red locks. "I just can't believe you of all people would disobey Makoto."

"What? And let this guy die?" Camila sneered. "Don't you get it? She had no choice."

Sage felt Mason stiffen beside her. She would have had a choice if his brother didn't stage the whole beat down. But when they asked what the hell a tiger Guardian was doing as her fake boyfriend, she left that part out.

"Still, we'd better tell Makoto. About this guy, I mean." Arielle glanced at AJ, laying on the ground beneath Caspar's feet. She gave a dramatic sigh and pulled out her phone. "I'll be the one to do it. The assignment was mine to lead, it's mine to report failure."

As soon as Arielle left the room, Camila muttered, "Crap leader if you ask me. We should have turned him ourselves, he would have been True then."

Caspar shook his head. "We never had the chance. He was turned as soon as his mark appeared. What more could we have done?"

"Actually telling Makoto straight away?" Nadya glared at Sage as she added, "Not keeping secrets."

Sage held back a smile. She couldn't help it. Nadya's judgmental face was exactly what she had envisioned. It didn't feel as bad as she thought it would, though. In fact, for once, Nadya's disapproval didn't bother her.

Nadya must have sensed the transformation in Sage, she blinked a few times quickly and looked away. "I knew I made the wrong choice by following Arielle's orders and now here we are cleaning up a mess we shouldn't have made."

Camila rolled her eyes. "Oh yeah, because you're the best Guardian there is. We are allowed to make mistakes Nadya, even you."

"I..." Nadya closed her eyes, brows dropping. She opened them again, a small tear resting in the corner. "I never said I was the best."

It was obvious that Nadya was sorry, but Camila didn't want to let it go. "But you act like it."

"All right. Enough!" Caspar huffed. "There's no point arguing." He waved his hand at AJ and then at Mason. "There are bigger problems here."

Mason twisted his body to Sage and whispered, "Is he talking about me? I'm a problem?"

The door swung open and Arielle walked in. "We have to meet Makoto in class. He said to bring both the Fallen."

"Mason isn't—" Sage began.

Nadya splayed her fingers and pushed her palm in Sage's direction. "Stop," she snapped. And then, her face softened. She turned her hand around, an offering for Sage to take. "You've done this alone long enough. We'll face the consequences together."

In the Shadow Society lecture room, Makoto stood over a still unconscious AJ, his eyes hooded with sadness. The recruits and Mason surrounded him, waiting for his orders. He looked up and as he noticed Mason, his pupils dilated.

"So, you're a Fallen?" he cried, storming closer. "Killing people and turning them against their will?"

"No sir." Mason shook his head wildly, taking a step back.

Makoto half-shifted, eyes a bright shade of gold. As he inched closer, Sage's heart kicked into overdrive. She knew his stance on the Fallen. It was his job to be rid of them. His job to kill them.

She leapt between them. "Please stop. He's not a Fallen."

Makoto stopped in his tracks and blinked. "And how would you know?"

She grasped Mason's hand, making sure he stayed behind her. "Because I turned him."

Makoto stared at Sage through his Guardian's golden eyes. His face didn't change as he asked, "You turned him?"

Sage took a few quick breaths. "I followed him to make sure he wouldn't bully anyone else and when I was satisfied others were safe, I left. But then, I felt called to go back. Like a tug. You told us that we should follow that tug, so I did. I went back and I found him beaten by his brother and dying. He already had a mark on him, so I turned him. To save him."

Silence fell across the room. Only the rattly breath of AJ could be heard.

Makoto shifted back to human form and nodded. "Good."

"Good?" Sage asked, letting Mason's hand go.

"Mmm." Makoto stepped back. He smiled at Mason. "Your father will be proud."

"You know my dad?" Mason gawked.

Makoto nodded once. "He asked me to bring you into the Shadow Society earlier this year. But I told him I couldn't, not until you had shown the signs of a True Guardian. I guess now you have."

"Are you kidding?" Arielle said. A certain bitterness laced her normally chipper voice. "We recite the rules every day for nothing?"

Makoto whipped his head in her direction. "Not for nothing." He forced himself to take a breath. Pointing at Sage, he said, "This, team, is what a successful solo assignment looks like. Congratulations, Sage. You are showing promising signs of being a stellar True Guardian."

"Sorry, what?" Nadya balked.

"Oh, didn't I teach you that? Sometimes assignments aren't given, they're aligned." Makoto chuckled to himself. "Honestly, it's my favorite part of the year, when recruits find this out on their own."

Sage's insides felt like goo. All this time she was worried about how he'd react, and he'd known about it all along. She pinched her leather necklace.

Makoto placed a warm hand around her shoulder.

"Some things are best experienced than taught. Always trust your instincts."

Sage closed her eyes, deciding right then and there to break the cycle inside her mind. She heard her mom's gentle voice as she said; "Sage Windsor, how many times have I told you to believe in yourself?"

Running her fingers over her necklace, Sage finally allowed herself to let go of her fear of trouble.

Camila cleared her throat, pointing to the elephant, or rather bear, in the room. "And, uh, AJ?"

Makoto frowned, glancing at AJ. "Yes, that. I need to consult with the Elders of the Veil."

Everyone rushed behind Makoto as he headed around his desk. Caspar ran to the back of the room and pressed a hidden button on the side of the projector. Above the board behind Makoto's desk, the projector lifted, and the wall moved with it. A small room about five meters square appeared beyond the wall. It was a secret compartment with long scratch marks dug in cement walls.

Makoto stepped inside. As the wall closed, he demanded, "No one is to go anywhere!"

"What the hell is happening?" Mason asked.

Sage thread her arm through his. With a teasing tone, she said, "You'll see."

# TWENTY FIVE

Caspar hit another button and the wall shimmered until it became transparent and everyone could see Makoto inside. He cracked his neck side to side, then fully shifted. A great wolf with black silky fur and eyes like the sun stood in his place.

"So," Sage said to Mason. "You know about the Veil?"

Staring at Makoto's wolf, Mason said, "It's where the Guardians are, waiting for us. Like an alternate dimension."

"Yeah, and we act as the conduit between dimensions. Did your dad ever tell you about what's beyond the in-between though?"

Mason shook his head. As if disappointed, he muttered, "No, he didn't."

"When we shift, we are joined to both the Veil *and* our world. But just as we can be human on this side, so can our animal. We just have to swap spots. They hold our place in this world as we go through theirs." She half-shifted, showing Mason her purple eyes.

Nodding at Makoto, she said, "Watch."

Mason half-shifted and cast his Veil-seeing eyes to

Makoto. The wolf's eyes flickered and the glow stopped. Beside the wolf, Makoto stood tall, his shape nothing but a transparent red aura. Makoto turned and walked on, shimmering through the wall until he couldn't be seen any longer. His wolf began to prowl. Its mouth raised to the ceiling as a howl broke out.

"And now his wolf is wild," Caspar added. "Hence the cage."

"Where's he going?" Mason asked, straining his Guardian's vision as if it could see that far into the Veil.

Sage explained, "To talk to the Elders of the Veil. They are who give us the assignments. They know things we don't."

"They'll help him weed out the Fallen on campus." Nadya said, shoulders slumping. "Well, they'd better."

Mason let out a nervous laugh. "Why the heck didn't you do that before? Save everyone attacking me, thinking I'm the culprit?"

"Apparently, we're not up to that part of training," Camila said, rolling her eyes.

Arielle shrugged, sauntering to Makoto's desk. "Anyway, Makoto says they speak in riddles and aren't always clear with their meanings. So, he only goes when it's necessary. Like now." She pulled his drawer open and sifted through his papers, lifting out one in particular.

"What are you doing?" Caspar asked.

Arielle waved the piece of paper, a wide grin on her face. She began reading, "Sage Windsor. Showing signs of secrecy and anti-Guardian behavior."

"What?" Sage leapt across the desk and ripped the note from Arielle. *Sage Windsor. Showing signs of being tasked her own assignment. Rule number three may be temporarily waived in this time.*

Mason stood behind her, reading over her shoulder. "Nice one, Floss. It says she was given her own assignment."

"This is lame." Camila huffed. "We should be doing

something. Getting out there and finding this Fallen. We should be fighting, not sitting back twiddling our thumbs."

For a moment Sage was hurt. She thought Camila was upset with her. It wasn't like she meant to have a solo assignment or that she inadvertently did the right thing by turning Mason.

Sage reached for Camila, clasping her wrist. "We'll get the Fallen. We just need to know who it is first. Isn't it better going in with our eyes wide open?"

"Now who's the perfect Guardian?" Camila mocked, articulating every consonant. "I'm going to take action. Are you coming?"

Sage refused to be offended. She understood Camila better than anyone. She was cruel when she felt inadequate. But now wasn't the time to prove themselves. And since she knew she'd done the right thing with Mason, she wasn't about to ruin it by being reckless with a Fallen. "We should stay here. Until Makoto returns."

"Suit yourself." Camila slid her hand out of Sage's grasp and a smooth bump tickled Sage's palm.

Sage glanced at Camila's hand to see a mood ring on her thumb. Camila spun around and marched to the door, her wavy brown hair swinging behind her. As she put her hand around the door handle, Mason pointed, mouth agape.

The door slammed behind her.

Arielle blew a raspberry and swiped the note from Sage. As she piled all of Makoto's papers back into his drawer, she said, "What's her problem?"

Still pointing to the now closed door, Mason gasped, "Oh my god. That's her. I've seen her somewhere before."

Sage knew he'd seen the mood ring. He'd seen her brown hair. He was placing her at a scene that was impossible for Sage to fathom. In an effort to stop him from accusing Camila of something she would never do, Sage offered, "In the courtyard. When you bumped

155

into me?"

"No," Mason replied, staring at the door.

"In the library?" Nadya offered. "When she pulled you off AJ?"

"No, before that. Last week." Mason faced Sage, his eyes lit up like a street lamp. "She's the one who bumped into me at the bar. She's the one who marked me."

Arielle bounded around the desk. "Did she touch you?"

Mason glanced at her, then to Caspar, to Nadya, to Sage. "Yeah, she grabbed my arm as she walked past me. She had a mood ring on her thumb. I turned to see who it was but could only see her brown wavy hair as she walked away." He threw his arm at the door. "Exactly like that."

"Brown wavy hair isn't uncommon. And tons of people have mood rings," Sage argued.

"Don't be naive, Sage," Arielle said, moving in front of Mason. She lifted his sleeve to reveal his mark. "This is where she touched you?"

Mason nodded.

Nadya shuffled in closer, peering at Mason's mark. "Camila touched AJ, too. In the library. Her name was on his list."

Caspar joined them next. They all closed in on Mason, believing the outrageous story. Sage felt like the room was spinning and time was moving too fast.

"Hold up now," she blurted. "You can't possibly think she marked them both? Camila? You've got to be kidding. She wouldn't—"

"Oh my god!" Arielle interrupted, her wide eyes falling on Sage. "She's always talking about how great it would be to turn someone. Remember, I warned you about it. Do you think she's a Fallen and that's why AJ is?"

"No!" Sage urged. "She isn't a Fallen. She's my best friend, I'm sure I'd know."

Caspar gave Sage a sad smile. "Makoto says that

they are great at deception."

Sage felt sick. She couldn't believe what she was hearing. Camila was a rebel who hated rules and always wanted to do things against Makoto, but she wasn't a Fallen. She couldn't be. Could she? Sage's knees buckled beneath her and Mason grabbed her around the waist to help her stay upright.

"I don't know but we need to get her," Caspar declared, already heading for the door.

Sage breathed in and out. Too quick. She clutched Mason as if she'd fall through the floor if she let go.

Nadya rubbed Sage's arm. "Don't worry. We'll take care of it."

Sage shook her head. They had to be wrong. There was no way she'd let them *take care of it*. Nadya had always had it in for Camila, any excuse to bring her down.

"Wait." She cried, regaining her composure. "I'll try and call her first, she doesn't know we're onto her."

# TWENTY SIX

Sage pulled out her phone, intent on warning Camila about the impending onslaught but there was no answer.

Arielle made herself comfortable on Makoto's chair. Kicking her heels onto his desk, she asked, "Do you think she killed that boy, too?"

"Not the Camila I know," Sage said, staring at her phone and watching it ring out again.

Nadya shared a glance with Caspar. "The Fallen are great at deception."

"Stop saying that!" Sage snapped.

Arielle rolled her bottom lip out, her wide eyes blinking with dramatic sadness. "It must be so hard to face the fact that someone you know and love isn't who they say they are. I'm really sorry, Sage. There's just too many signs—"

Arielle's blasé and forever perky attitude was starting to get to Sage. Her voice was all bite as she said, "Camila is a rebel but she isn't a killer."

"I'm sorry." Mason tried to sympathize. "But it was her. I'm sure of it."

Sage felt like her insides were ripping apart. How could she have missed it? Was she blind? Was she a terrible judge of character? She backed away from everyone. "There must be some mistake. Some good explanation."

Caspar clapped his hands together. "If she isn't answering her phone, I think we should go find her. We'll bring her back here to Makoto. He'll find out the truth."

"No!" Sage shouted, her whole body shaking. "He'll kill her. We can't let him kill her."

An unusual high-pitched peep flew out of Nadya's mouth. "I'm sure he wouldn't do that. There must be something else he could do..."

"No, he will," Arielle stated, rolling Makoto's pen through her fingers. "Once a Fallen, always a Fallen."

She said it so flippantly that Sage wanted to punch her square in the face. Mason glided his hand over her bunching fist. She didn't know when he had moved beside her.

"Breathe," he said, softly. "Getting mad won't help you."

In her other hand, Sage's phone buzzed. As everyone turned their attention to her, her heart flipped. She lifted it and stared at the screen.

"Who is it?" Nadya asked.

Arielle swung around in Makoto's chair and stood. "It's her isn't it?"

Before Sage could even decide what to say, Nadya snatched the phone. She boomed into the receiver, "Where the hell are you?" She glanced at Sage. "Yes, she's okay.... No, of course I wouldn't hurt... Hey, listen, we know the truth about you. If you give yourself up now, we'll... hello? Hello."

"Great," Arielle said, snatching the phone. "Now you've scared her off."

Sage's knees gave way and she collapsed onto the ground. She felt numb as Mason pried the phone from Arielle's grasp and held it out for her. She took it slowly.

Mason slumped next to her. "What are we going to

do?"

"We have to find her," Arielle commanded. "Bring her to justice."

"All right, this is Camila we're talking about," Caspar kept his voice even. "We want her caught but I'm sure none of us want to see her hurt."

He glared at Nadya when he said the last part, as if calling her out. Her eyes found the ground. She mumbled, "We need to tell Makoto."

Arielle cringed, "I don't know if that's a great idea —"

Nadya snapped her eyes up. "You know none of this would have happened if we went to him at the start? If we told him about AJ." She glanced at Sage. "And if you told him about Mason. Maybe we could have stopped Camila before she went off the deep end."

Sage bit her lip to stop the tears from falling. Her eyes stung. Her chest ached. She didn't want to believe it, but it all made too much sense. The way Camila was so desperate to turn someone. That look in her eye was a dead give-away and all Sage did was brush it off as Camila being Camila. That wouldn't have helped anything.

The proof defeated her heart. She finally said, "By the time they were marked she was already lost."

Nadya's face softened. She helped Sage up. "Do you want to us to take care of it while you sit this one out?"

The way she looked at Sage with sympathy would have been nice if it didn't come with so much confusion and pain. Sage shook her head. "I'm coming."

As Caspar and Nadya headed for the door, Sage reached back for Mason's hand. He stood begrudgingly mouthing the words, "I'm sorry." Sage grimaced and dragged him out of the classroom.

"I'll stay here then," Arielle called. "You know, watch AJ and release Makoto when he gets back."

160

The corridor was eerily quiet for that time of day. Last period would normally have ended with students milling to their lockers. But instead, they were all huddled in their rooms, looking out their windows for wild cougars or bears.

As they left the building and wandered down the cobblestone path, Nadya said, "Sage, I'm sorry. I acted out of line before, taking your phone. It was hasty and didn't do any of us any favors. Maybe you could try calling her again? She's never liked us but she seems to adore you."

Sage nodded. Her hands shook. But even though everything inside her screamed that it was wrong, she lifted her phone and dialed the number.

"Back off Nadya, you self righteous—"

"It's me," Sage interrupted. Stopping, she turned away from Caspar, Nadya, and Mason. "Just me."

Silence.

"Camila, where are you?"

"Are you coming to help me or accuse me?" Camila huffed.

Sage couldn't answer without lying. So, she asked, "What do you need help with?"

There was a long pause before Camila replied, "I'm at the edge of the forest behind the dorms... I was going to search for those missing varsity boys."

Camila trusted her. Sudden doubt crept in. Had she done the right thing? Looking out at the winding driveway. The evidence played out. Camila was the one who marked Mason. She was always going on about turning people. She'd hardly listen to Makoto's intricate lessons and want to skip ahead to the in-depth stuff, the dangerous stuff. Sage couldn't deny it any longer.

"Okay, wait there. I'll meet you in a minute."

As she ended the call, Mason cupped her shoulder. "Are you all right?"

Sage didn't know. A numbness engulfed her whole being. She gave a curt shrug and said, "I'm stupid for believing in her all this time."

"You're far from stupid." He ran his thumb over her cheek. "Where is she?"

Sage turned to Nadya and Caspar. Without emotion, Sage replied, "Behind the dorms."

# TWENTY SEVEN

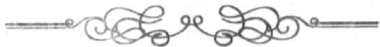

The four of them ran across the oval. Gravel crunched beneath their feet as they hit the parking lot. Tire marks of the ambulances were all that remained of AJ's earlier attack. Sage tried to stay ahead of everyone, just in case.

Camila squinted as she saw them all approaching. "I didn't expect the whole gang to —

"Stop it, Camila," Nadya broke out in front of Sage. "We know what you are. We know what you've done."

Camila brought her hands on her hips. "And what's that exactly?"

"Let's not make a scene." Nadya reached for her.

Camila snatched her hand away and stepped back. With her chin lifted, she said, "Tell me what I've done? Is it as bad as being a self-righteous bitch who sucks up to the teacher to advance herself?" She moved her glare to Caspar. "Or a dumb sidekick, who pretends to care but bad mouths us all behind our backs?"

"Ouch." Caspar clutched his chest.

Camila's eyes moved to Sage. "Or keeping a secret, like turning a boy?"

The venom in her tone stung. And it was then that Sage knew her worst fears had come true. Camila was a Fallen.

"You really want us to list them?" Nadya said, her eyes flashing neon blue. "Marking innocents without their consent? Killing Mal. Turning AJ into a murderous Guardian?"

Camila's face dropped. "What? You think I'm..." she stared at Sage with sadness. "Do you believe this crap they're spinning? You're my best friend. You know me. Tell them I wouldn't. Sage?"

Hesitating, Sage stuttered, "I... I don't know."

A tear fell down Camila's face. As the salty droplet hit her mouth, she licked her lips. "Okay, fine. I marked AJ. Is that what you want to hear?"

"Finally!" Nadya threw her hands in the air. "That's some truth, now how about the rest?"

Camila snarled at Nadya, "But I did not mark Mason. I did not kill that boy. And I did not turn AJ."

The flicker of hope that had remained in Sage reignited. Deep in her heart, she knew the truth. Camila would never hurt anyone.

Camila continued, "I just wanted some excitement you know? I figured, I'd mark him, maybe lure some Fallen to the school. I was going to give him my blood to cure him, while we went on a mission to find some real Fallen. I just wanted to do something, anything with meaning."

"Come on." Caspar's voice was soothing. He took a few slow steps toward her. As he took a hold of her elbow, he said, "The game is up, Camila."

"Sage," Camila pleaded, not fighting against Caspar. Tears rolled down her cheeks in waves. "I would never kill someone. You have to believe me."

"I believe you," Sage whispered to herself. She took a breath as her instincts pushed the truth from her heart to her mind. Louder, she said, "I believe you."

Behind them, a cackle rose. "Oh my god, you guys are hilarious."

Spinning around, Sage saw Arielle strolling over. AJ stalked behind her, eyes wild.

"Arielle!" Nadya cried. "Look out!"

Giggling, Arielle glanced over her shoulder. She threw a thumb in AJ's direction. "Oh, don't worry, he won't hurt me. I'm his Alpha."

Nadya gasped. "But the only way you could be his Alpha is if he's in your clan or..."

Arielle's mouth fell open, she lifted her delicate fingers and covered her mouth. "Go on."

Nadya's brow wrinkled. "Or if you turned him."

"Bingo," Arielle proclaimed, rolling her eyes to the heavens. "You're so slow. Such an easy bunch of morons to manipulate. I don't even know if I've had fun." She stopped walking just shy of the parking lot's edge, keeping enough distance between them. "Well, I think I've had fun. The way you hate each other is quite comical. The way you work as the most pathetic team in existence. The way you lie and weasel your way into believing you're going to be such wonderful True Guardians. Hil.ar.ious."

Arielle took something from AJ. From where Sage stood, it looked like a chocolate colored scarf, but as Arielle placed it on her head, she realized exactly what it was. A wig.

"Like my hair, Mason?" Arielle teased. She flicked the strands over her shoulder, before ripping the wig off and throwing it to ground. Looking at Camila, she blinked innocently. "Can I have my ring back now, please?"

"You're the..." Mason stammered. "You're the one who marked me?"

"Oh. Em. Gee." Arielle slammed her hands to her knees. "You're all killing me. You should see your faces. This is better than I thought it would be."

Caspar released Camila. "It was you all along wasn't it?"

"Ooh." Arielle squeezed her fists in front of her in excitement. "I've had such a good time playing with you guys. I knew Mason was the assignment the whole time, considering I was the one who made the deal with his brother to turn them both. I had to get you off the scent somehow."

"What?" Mason gasped.

"Oh yeah, your brother came to me a while ago. He knew the only way to become a Guardian was to do it the easy way. With a Fallen. We figured I'd turn you first and from there it would be easy to convince you to turn him. He didn't want to do it without you, isn't that sweet?"

Sage felt rage burn her insides. It wasn't just her that was manipulated, it was Mason, too. She scowled, "You're sick."

Arielle tilted her head and gave a sweet smile. "You guys bought into the AJ story so easily. Camila, your little surprise with marking him threw me off but I used it to my advantage." Her eyes scanned hungrily over Mason. "Shame I couldn't turn that hottie, though. You were too quick for me, Sagey."

"Arielle?" Camila spoke up, moving next to Sage. "Where's Makoto?"

"In the cage." Arielle's innocent smile twisted into a menacing smirk.

Beside Arielle, AJ hopped between his feet. "Can we kill them now?"

She threw her arm across his chest, stopping him in his tracks. "Patience, my little protegé. All in good time. You need to savor these moments. I mean, just look at their faces. Don't they give you life?"

Caspar took a place next to Mason and Nadya soon followed him. The five of them stood in a line, from Camila to Nadya, facing Arielle and AJ. Nadya said, "You killed Mal? Where are Ethan and Brian?"

"Well, I didn't want to," Arielle pouted, "But he wasn't making a very good Fallen. He kept crying and saying how much the fangs hurt when they grew. Such a sook. But the others?" Her eyes darkened and she nodded at something behind them.

Sage turned to see the two boys from the varsity team step out of the wood. Muscles grew upon muscles. And they were grinning, eager for a fight.

"Take them down," Arielle ordered.

For a moment, Sage felt her heart leave her body. But when Ethan shifted into a wolf, she came plummeting back down to earth. He prowled toward them, his sight set firmly on Camila at the end of the line.

Suddenly nothing else mattered. Ethan leapt and Sage cried, "Watch out, behind you!"

As Camila spun, she instinctively half-shifted. She grabbed the bounding wolf by its neck and sunk her claws into its skin. She held him there for a moment, his blood dripping down her arm, before throwing him back into the forest.

Running after Ethan, she yelled, "We have to take the fight out of sight."

In front of them, Brian shifted into a lion. One moment he was pacing impatiently and the next, he was lurching for them at full speed. Caspar shifted next. His wolf's eyes looked almost metallic blue as he placed himself in front of his friends. Brian greeted him by clamping his jaw around Caspar's leg.

"Get off him!' Nadya yelled, allowing her fox to take over. She bowled into the lion, knocking him off Caspar. Once Ethan stumbled back, Caspar and Nadya ran into the forest to lure him away.

While the three of them dealt with the varsity boys in the forest, Sage prepared herself to face Arielle. She grabbed Mason by the wrist and turned around. Nothing but two dormitories, a parking lot, and a barren field of overgrown grass and patches of mud remained. Arielle and AJ had gone.

"Sage!" Caspar yelled at the same time a thump of footsteps galloped from the forest.

Ethan's lion, although scratched, tore across the ground toward them. Behind him, Caspar panted against a tree, blood pouring from his forehead. The sight of him injured infuriated her. How dare someone hurt a person she cared for. She shifted into her owl and Mason half-shifted beside her.

"I'll do what I do best," she said, flying in a straight line for the lion.

She interrupted its run, dancing her feet over its face. She could never take down a lion. Not half-shifted. Not even fully shifted. But she could distract it.

As Brian opened his jaw to crunch her body whole, a whir from the side—a bright and glorious red—took the lion out. Brian, unconscious, reverted to human form. Fully shifted into his tiger, Mason crouched over him. He held Brian him down, one paw on either side of his body.

Camila hobbled back, her face was bruised and she winced with every step. Sage, now human, ran to greet her. "I'm so sorry for doubting you."

"It's okay. I didn't give you much reason to trust me. You told me your secret—I should have told you mine." As Camila spoke, she lifted her hand and twisted the mood ring off her thumb. Ethan's blood stained the obsidian stone. She tossed it onto the ground. "Arielle gave it to me the day we got the assignment. I thought it was a gift, not a tool to frame me."

"What do I do?" Mason asked, still fully shifted.

Caspar rushed over, his arm around Nadya, helping her walk. Blood poured from her kneecap, coating her shin in red. They stood back, staring at Mason, waiting for him to do the inevitable.

"I don't want to kill him." Mason's voice quivered.

Sage rushed over and knelt beside him. "He's a Fallen, we have to."

"There's no other way," Camila offered. "I just killed Ethan. I didn't want to but imagine how many innocent people will die at his hands."

Mason grimaced.

Nadya crouched opposite him, hissing through her

teeth as the scratch mark on her knee opened up. She let her fingers glide through Brian's hair. Sighing, she said, "Think of it this way, we'll be doing him a favor. He's in turmoil now—Fallen venom ripping through his veins. He will never be the same."

"You do it then." Mason half-shifted back. He stood and held out his hands in front of himself, watching his claws retract.

Nadya sat upright, moving her head above the boy's. She licked her lips and hovered her hands around his neck—not quite touching. She stayed that way for a while, breath shaking.

"Do you need me to do it?" Caspar asked.

As soon as he said the words, Nadya collapsed back and whipped her hands to her side. She rolled to her feet, making way for Caspar.

He stood in her place and took a deep breath. "Brian is my brother's team-mate."

"Oh, for god's sake," Camila huffed. She pushed Caspar out of the way and without even shifting at all, she splayed her fingers and grabbed Brian's face.

As Camila twisted his head to the side, Sage turned away. She faced Mason, watching his eyes take in the scene. The sound of a neck snapping made his eyes glaze over, he blinked and met her gaze. One quick exhale to tell her it was over.

He said, "This isn't anything like I thought it would be."

"You and me both," Camila replied, pulling her blazer sleeves over her crimson stained hands.

"Guys," Nadya said, rubbing dried blood off her healed wound. "We need to get Makoto."

# TWENTY EIGHT

They ran into the Shadow Society lecture room and found Makoto in his human form pacing in the cage. As Casper ran to open the wall, Sage turned to Mason. "Do your fangs hurt when they grow?"

He shook his head. "Not at all."

"It must be a Fallen thing," Camila said. "And in case you're wondering, no, mine don't hurt either."

The wall retracted and Makoto stormed out. His wild eyes landed on each of them. "Where's Arielle?"

Nadya waved her hand. "Off doing villainy things, I assume."

Makoto clenched his teeth. He marched to his desk and whipped out a map of the school. "We'll need to shut her down immediately."

He pointed to the boys' dorm. "I'll do a varsity team head count. She'll be after strong people to join her. I'm assuming those boys that went missing are hers already?"

"Uhhh." Caspar winced. "We found them. Camila took care of them."

Makoto glanced at Camila, a softness falling over his face. "I'm not surprised."

Camila swallowed and gave a sad smile. "We hid the bodies in the forest. Will probably need to dispose of them properly."

Nodding, Makoto turned back to the map. He took a long breath out and hung his head. "This is the first time the school's been attacked. I made a mistake with her."

Sage stepped forward, now knowing the burden and responsibility of turning someone. "You weren't to know she'd be a Fallen."

Makoto pressed his hands onto the map and sighed. The recruits gathered around their broken-hearted teacher, silent and waiting. Makoto sniffed and stood up straight.

"We have to work quickly. Caspar, I'm sure you're worried about your brother. I suggest you find him and see if he's been marked. Get as much information from him about the team as possible. Nadya, I need you to get into the office and find me a list of the team. Camila, you're with me. We're going to gather them up and bring them here. If they've been marked and haven't been turned we can at least stop her in her tracks."

"But if we can't find her, how will you cure them?" Nadya asked.

Makoto's lips upturned. "You think those blood tests at the start of semester were to test for any vitamin deficiencies?" He walked around his desk, opened the bottom drawer, and pulled out vial with Arielle's name on it.

Sage asked, "And what do we do? Look for her?"

Makoto shook his head. He pointed the vial at Mason. "It seems your assignment isn't over, Sage. There's unfinished business."

"The assignment?" Sage shook her head. "Is that more important than finding Arielle?"

"We can handle her. But your assignment is pressing. I think you'll find it's all interconnected." Makoto slammed his drawer shut. He cast his eyes on Mason. "There's a new development isn't there?"

Sage felt Mason tense beside her. He gave a small

nod. "My brother's been marked, I'm assuming by Arielle."

Camila raised her hands in surrender. "I didn't mark anyone except AJ, I swear."

Makoto's brow lowered. "We'll talk about that later. Now, come with me." As he headed for the door, he called over his shoulder, "Bring Ben here, we'll give him the cure."

The four of them rushed out of the room, leaving Sage and Mason. She grabbed his hand and marched for the door. "Let's go save your brother."

"Whoa!" Mason declared, resisting Sage's strength. "I thought you said I needed to kick him out of my life?"

Sage shook her head. "I gave you the wrong advice. I gave you advice based on my life... not yours."

Mason frowned. "What do you mean?"

"I told you to walk away. But maybe what he needs most..." Sage gazed at Mason intensely, his gorgeous face lined with confusion, "is you."

# TWENTY NINE

"Something isn't right," Mason said as they approached the boxing studio. "The sign isn't on."

Sage glanced above the door. He was right, it wasn't lit. She shrugged. "Maybe he forgot."

Mason glared at her. "You don't get it. Ben never forgets anything. He's meticulous. Something's wrong."

He rushed to the window and peered in. Sage hurried to catch up, standing on her tip-toes to see through. Inside the boxing ring, three men were tied to chairs. One of them was Ben. The other two were on the varsity team. Arielle paced around the unconscious trio, eyes ablaze.

"They look drugged," Mason stated, his whole body tensing.

"No, don't you remember?" Sage whispered. "It's transition. They seem sick as the mark works its way through them. She's waiting for it to appear so she can turn them."

Mason's hands clenched into fists. He moaned, "Why?"

She knew it was a rhetorical question, but answered anyway. "Extra strength. Her Guardian's a small domestic-looking cat, she wants big cats or wolves or bears."

"We should call for backup." Mason patted his pockets. "I don't have my phone."

As Sage took hers out of her blazer, she had a thought. "Do you think Makoto knew she was here?"

Mason turned back to the window. "You think he wants us to take her down on our own?"

"I don't know," Sage replied.

With shaking fingers Sage typed a rushed message to Makoto: *She's at the boxing studio in Burrville. Please hurry.*

"Sage?" Mason's voice was a warning.

She peered through the window, seeing Arielle hover over Ben. She held his shirt up, baring his stomach. A black spiral shimmered beside his belly button. Arielle cracked her knuckles.

Sage gasped. "She's going to turn him."

"He can't be a Fallen!" Mason declared, already running for the door. He was inside before Sage had even taken a step to follow.

She quickly grabbed the steel bars covering the window and pulled herself closer to see. Arielle had half-shifted, her tiny fangs protruding through her lips. She was about to clamp her jaw around Ben when Mason charged in.

"Sorry, Mom," Sage muttered to herself. "I'm not staying out of trouble this time."

She pushed herself away from the window and ran for the door. Once inside the studio, she bolted to catch up to Mason.

Seeing them both, Arielle moaned and dropped Ben's shirt. "You've got to be kidding me."

"Stop, please," Mason begged. He moved slowly toward the ring, careful not to startle anyone.

Ben rolled his head around so he could see past Arielle. He rasped, "Don't fret, brother. I'll be all right. I want this."

A wide smile spread across Arielle's face.

"Trust me," Mason said, inching closer. Sage kept herself on his heels. "You don't want it. Not like this."

Arielle leapt to the edge of the ring, lip curling. "Back off."

Sage tugged on Mason's wrist, urging him to stop. Mason halted and tucked his chin over his shoulder. He whispered, "What if *I* turn him?"

Remembering Makoto's lesson on personality, she replied, "It takes a certain type of person to become a True Guardian. He might still be a Fallen. What if your father was right to worry?"

"Bite me, already!" Ben yelled, saliva spitting everywhere.

Arielle glowered and slipped away from the ropes, all too ready to comply with his wishes.

Sage pushed against Mason's back. She whispered loudly in his ear, "You save him while I distract her. Makoto has her blood, we can cure him."

Shifting into her owl, Sage flew around Mason and headed straight for Arielle. She clutched Arielle's collar with her talons and dragged her across the ring. Arielle flailed her arms, scratching at Sage's legs to let her go. A claw tore through Sage's wing, sending searing pain down her arm.

Half-shifting back, Sage collapsed to the floor. Her wings bunched beneath her as talons grew from the ends of her fingers. As blood dripped down her arm, she pressed her palm hard against the wound on her bicep. Arielle bared her fangs and crawled over Sage's body.

"That's all you're good for, Sagey. Just a distraction."

Arielle swiped at Sage's chest, her claws tearing through material and piercing skin. Over and over again, she scratched, burying her claws deeper every time. Sage screamed out in agony; shock, fear, and pain rendering her immovable. She felt warm blood as it dripped down her torso, making rivers in the divots of her ribs. The edges of her vision began to blur.

175

As Arielle lifted her bloody hand for one final blow, fingers curled around her wrist. Her body went flying over the ropes, across the room, and skidded into the stack of weights. Mason stood in Arielle's place, hand reaching for Sage.

The moment of reprieve sent cool healing to the cuts on her chest. She felt the wounds tingle as her skin sewed itself back together. She took a breath, and Mason's hand. As she stood, she noticed blood around his mouth.

She blinked and whipped her head across the ring. Ben slumped back in his chair as teeth marks healed around his mark. Through her half-shifted eyes, she could see his aura sparking green, and his jaguar Guardian moving beside him.

# THIRTY

"What have you done?" Arielle screamed, clambering to her feet. "He was mine!"

The door swung open and Sage hoped against all hope that it was Makoto coming to put an end to all this. But instead, AJ walked in. His blond hair fell over his eyes as he scanned the room. He took one look at Arielle and turned his glaring gaze to Mason.

"There's no bullying me now..." AJ motioned to his buffed up body.

Mason widened his stance, both fists at the ready. He growled, "I was never going to hurt you."

AJ shrugged, half-shifting into his bear.

Mason took a step in front of Sage. He wiped his mouth, streaking the back of his hand in blood. "But I'll hurt you now."

"Try." AJ lifted his hands and wiggled his fingers in a *come here* motion.

As Mason headed for AJ, a loud shriek resonated through the studio. Arielle brushed past Sage, throwing an unexpected fist against her temple. White dots sparked across her vision. Light-headed and knees buckling, Sage fell to the floor. As she caught her breath, she glanced up to see Arielle leaping onto Mason's back. Arielle wrapped her legs around his waist and clenched her fingers through his hair, bending his head back.

"Get him!" she commanded.

AJ's eyes flashed orange and he rolled his neck. "With pleasure."

AJ swung his open hand, slapping hard against Mason's jaw. Mason stumbled and the weight of Arielle on his back sent them colliding into the bars in the middle of the room. Arielle's head smacked hard against metal and her eyes rolled to the ceiling. Her limbs falling limp, she released her hold on Mason and tumbled to the floor. Sage felt her mind clear, silently praising her body for its fast healing capabilities. She reached for the ropes of the ring and pulled herself up.

With Arielle now off his back, Mason shook his body and steadied himself. The fall had made his Guardian retreat, returning him to human form. He heaved a weighted bar over Arielle's body to keep her in place. Opposite him, AJ stared wildly at his trapped Alpha. He growled and lunged for Mason, throwing his fist in a wide swing. With no time to shift, Mason dodged the punch and jabbed his knuckles hard into AJ's gut.

AJ doubled over, gasping for air. Mason grabbed his shoulders and quickly jolted his knee up. It connected with AJ's chin and the impact sent him barreling to the floor.

Grinning, Mason turned to Sage. "Remember my lesson on finding weakness?" Tapping his head, he said, "Strong but slow. I didn't even need to shift."

AJ flipped his head up and bared his fangs. Still on the ground, he reached for Mason's leg and clutched his ankle, ripping his foot from under him. Mason joined him on the floor.

Sage jolted to life. She glanced around the room. Arielle was knocked out. Ben was sleeping. The other two marked boxers were tied up. And AJ was climbing to his feet.

Mason writhed on the cement, a patch of blood coating his eyebrow. His arms shook as he tried to help himself up. Sage panicked. She needed to help him. But how? A distraction, again? Is that all she was good for?

"Let me help you up," AJ jeered as he thrust his fingers around Mason's throat. He lifted him up until Mason's feet dangled above the floor.

"Stop!" Sage cried.

AJ gave her a side-eye. He scoffed and turned his attention back to Mason, squeezing tighter. Mason's eyes flashed red and he half-shifted, digging his claws into AJ's fist. Wincing, AJ released his hold and swung his other arm around. His fist connected with Mason's jaw—the collision knocking him out instantly.

Sage jumped through the ring to the ground. "Mason!"

AJ flung his head around, rage in his eyes.

It was just her. It was all left to her. A mere distraction wouldn't cut it this time.

In a heartbeat, she shifted and flew back through the ropes into the ring. AJ's bear chased after her headfirst through the ropes, but as he leapt up onto the ring, his back legs became tangled. As he thrashed to get loose, Sage wasted no time to rush toward him feet first. She scratched at his face, aiming for his eyes.

AJ kicked his legs free and lunged, snapping his jaw. His teeth scraped through the tips of her wings and tore a cluster of feathers out from their roots. As he spat them on the ground, pain soared down her arm.

*I will heal,* she convinced herself. Forcing her wings in motion, she moved forward and swiped at his face again. In one swift movement, he swatted at her small owl. His paw thumped against her body and she tumbled across the ring, skidding to the other side. Wheezing, she flipped herself upright.

AJ bounded for her.

Sage wasn't a carnivore or a beast. She knew that she didn't have the strength to beat him, not even if she half-shifted. But she was small, she was svelte, and she was nimble. They weren't great odds, but it was something.

Grimacing through the pain, she spread her wings and lifted off the floor. AJ's large bear shook the ring as he took a leap for her. Still in the air, she tucked her wings and legs into her body and rolled to the side. AJ swept right past her, breaking through the ropes as though they were soft spaghetti. As soon as he landed on the ground, he spun around, eyes on Sage.

She squared herself up again, not daring to let him out of sight. AJ leapt into the ring and landed with a thud. He spread his claws and swiped. Sage rolled again, dodging his attack.

A frustrated growl rumbled from AJ's throat that rippled around the studio. He swiped again. She ducked and rolled. But this time, he was waiting. As she flitted away from his paw, AJ widened his mouth and pounced. He clamped down—half her body caught in his mouth.

A vile tang wafted from his mouth as saliva coated her body and one of her wings. It took her a moment to realize it was her own blood she could smell. The sting of teeth piercing skin was enough to render a normal human unconscious. But Sage wasn't a normal human. She was a freaking owl Guardian.

She craned her neck as far as it could go. Mason was still on the ground, sleeping as peacefully as he had when she first turned him. On the other side of the studio, Arielle was unconscious too, trapped under a hundred pound weight. It was up to her to take AJ down. She had to; she had no other choice.

Against her body's initial desire to recoil, Sage pushed her wing further inside AJ's mouth and grazed the top of his palete. He buckled, and as his jaw twitched, she slid her legs free. AJ growled and clamped her wing between his teeth.

This was it, do or die. She flicked her legs, aiming her talons for his throat but she couldn't reach. AJ huffed, his delighted eyes bearing down on her.

She couldn't get away, she'd accepted that. But there was no way she'd let a Fallen win. How many more people would die?

Only her. She decided.

Sage ran the end feather of her wing along his palete again and this time when he twitched, she swiveled the position of her body inside his mouth. He clamped down, enveloping her neck. As teeth the size of daggers pierced her small owl, she swung her legs forward. Sage felt the warmth of his skin as her talons just missed their target. Her body was hot and wet and tearing in two but again, she swung. As AJ forced his jaw down, she pushed into the bite.

One of her talons hit his skin. She hooked it into his flesh and dragged it along his neck. Deep enough.

She released her talon and let the searing agony take over her body. As Sage hung limp, her body tearing in half, the sound of gurgling liquid rose in AJ's throat. His jaw slacked and he spat her out with the blood. She fell to the floor, her critical wounds instinctively shifting her back into human form.

AJ transformed, too. He collapsed in a heap, a stream of blood pouring from his neck. His head tilted back, hollow eyes glaring at Sage. He blinked once, twice, and then no more.

She wasn't sure in that moment, what her assignment actually was. To turn Mason. To stop Ben becoming a Fallen. To stop Arielle. Or even AJ. Either way, in that moment, she knew it was done.

As she stared into AJ's lifeless eyes, darkness vignetted her vision; and everything went black.

# THIRTY ONE

Sage stirred. As she woke, her whole body ached as though she was held by a tightening vice. A wet cloth pressed against her collarbone, it dabbed across her shoulder and down her arm. Memories of why she hurt rushed to the surface. She opened her eyes and inhaled a fierce amount of air.

Makoto crouched over her, wiping her wounds with a towel. His eyes crinkled into a smile. "There she is."

She strained to sit up, but Makoto pushed her back down. "You've been through a lot. Let your body heal."

Sage was laying at the edge of the ring in the same spot where she fell. AJ had been moved—in his place was a stain of crimson, glistening under the fluorescent lights of the studio. Arielle had been tied to a chair next to a still sleeping Ben. She stared at Sage, her short red hair hanging in strands around her scowling face.

Outside the ring, Caspar and Nadya were coating the spiral marks of the two varsity boys with a pinkish white ointment. Sage assumed it was the cure, which meant they hadn't been turned yet. Somewhat of a relief.

Craning her neck, she searched the room. "Mason?"

Makoto leaned out of the way and revealed Mason, sitting against the steel beam in the middle of the studio. His arms hung over his lifted knees, head hanging low. He turned his face, wet from tears, and glanced her way.

Sage's heart sank. She knew what it felt like to make the decision to turn someone. The look in his eyes swept her back to the night she did the same thing to him.

But a hint of fear shadowed over him, too. No matter who Ben was turned by, there seemed to be an overwhelming risk that he would become Fallen anyway. Because of Mason though, he had more of a chance of becoming True.

Time would tell.

Sage's eyes fell to Arielle. Blinking slowly, she asked Makoto, "Did you know that she'd be here?"

He shook his head. "The Elders always speaks in riddles. *Sage is the only one who can stop it,* was all I got from them. But it makes sense now, that it was your assignment to complete it alone."

"You're such a bad ass," Camila's voice shrieked from the side. She ran to the edge of the ring and clutched at the ropes. "Such a freaking bad ass."

Makoto helped Sage sit up and she checked on her wounds. Only dried blood remained. She took a deep breath and smiled.

As the thought of Arielle's marking spree hit, her smile faded. "What are we going to do with the Fallen?"

Makoto opened his mouth to speak but Camila climbed through the ropes and skidded alongside Sage. She pointed to Arielle and Ben. "These two are the only ones left. We managed to cure all the varsity team she'd marked."

Sage hesitated to ask, "What are we going to do with them?"

The Shadow Society - Elle Scott

"Uh," Camila raised her brows. "The obvious."

Sage swallowed and spun to face Makoto. "We don't know if Ben's Fallen, though. Mason turned him, just in case."

Makoto winced and averted his gaze.

"Makoto?" Sage pleaded. "What are we going to do with them?"

An emphatic "No" echoed around the studio. Mason leapt through the ropes and stood in front of Ben. "You can't kill him!"

Camila glowered at Arielle. "I'm sure it wouldn't be too hard to kill *her*."

Arielle sat up straight, her head tilting like an innocent puppy. She fluttered her large brown eyes. "Aww, kill me? But you're my bestie."

Taking a threatening step, Camila raised her fist. "Can I do it now?"

An unmistakable look of fear washed over Arielle's face. She clenched her jaw and lowered her gaze. Her thumb ran over the rope that tied her wrists.

Makoto took a deep breath and stood up. "It's what I've always done. There's no cure for the Fallen. They'll always have the urge to kill."

Mason shared a worried glance with Sage and raked his hands through his hair. "There has to be another way. We don't even know if he's Fallen yet."

"Okay. We'll wait," Makoto said, a twinge of frustration in his voice. "But you're responsible for him. The Fallen are great at deception so you'll need to be on your A game."

"I will." Mason nodded eagerly. "I have to. He's my brother."

Makoto shook his head. "I have siblings, too. One is..." he snapped his mouth shut, sucked his bottom lip, then said, "Let's just say, I understand. But trust me, sometimes it's easier to cut your losses before he loses control."

The studio fell silent. All eyes on Mason. He was stuck in an impossible situation. Even Arielle turned her attention to him, her piercing eyes glaring through strands of matted hair.

Mason sniffed at the same time Nadya climbed into the ring. She moved slowly—carefully—a rare peace-keeping smile on her face. "We'll all help you," she offered. "We can make sure he stays True. As a team... as a clan."

Caspar followed her in. He held out an empty vial and passed it to Makoto. "Their marks have disappeared."

"Good," Makoto said, slipping the vial into his jacket pocket. "That's all of them accounted for."

Arielle huffed. She slumped in her seat, the look of disappointment hitting her face. Like she was a birthday girl who asked for a Rolls Royce but ended up with a Go-Kart.

"What now?" Nadya asked.

Makoto glanced at Arielle. She immediately began squirming in her seat. "Please, Makoto. I don't wanna die. I haven't killed anyone... no one innocent, anyway. I just... I couldn't..." Her forehead wrinkled. "I couldn't help it."

Sage studied Arielle and a twinge of sorrow tugged at her heart strings. The thought of killing her seemed so brutal. It was easier with AJ, she was fighting for her life. But Arielle was tied up, it didn't seem fair. Even the worst of humans still got jail time.

Makoto closed his eyes, a growl rumbling in the base of his throat. When he opened his eyes again, they flashed gold. He snapped, "You don't get to beg for your life, Fallen."

Sage jumped, shocked at Makoto's outburst. Surely, as a Guardian, they were supposed to care for everyone, not just the good. She tried to remain diplomatic as she asked, "You aren't really going to kill her, are you?"

Without taking his eyes off Arielle, Makoto flung his arm in her direction. "This is a life lesson, students. The Fallen will deceive. You just need to have enough strength to deal with it before it's too late."

Arielle's chin quivered. Her voice was barely a whisper, "Please, don't kill me."

Makoto craned his neck and looked to the ceiling. "Dammit."

His hesitation settled Sage's mind. He didn't want to kill her, either. But he felt it was his duty.

"You need me to do it?" Camila offered.

A strong hand raised in her direction. Makoto demanded, "No one kills her. She'll remain in the cell. Until we figure out a way to deal with her."

Sage sighed. So did Arielle. There had to be another way.

Camila must have heard; she turned to Sage and offered her hand. Sage took Camila's help and stood. She wrapped her arms around her best friend, mumbling into her hair, "I think you're pretty bad ass, too."

As they turned to face the others, Camila kept her arm draped over Sage's shoulders, and said, "Either way, Makoto, it seems you're a student down."

Makoto sighed, his shoulders rising and falling dramatically. He looked around the room, at Caspar and Nadya, Camila and Sage, and finally at Mason. "I don't think so. I have five. The perfect number."

Mason's mouth dropped open. He glanced at Sage then back to Makoto about three times over. "You're inviting me into the society?"

Makoto let a small smirk lift his lips, and the slightest nod of his head was all the answer Mason needed.

# THIRTY TWO

Sage swung her leg off Mason's bike and her boots landed on the drying soil. She took a deep breath in, allowing the scent of the forest to surround her whole being. She felt different, changed. As though the person she truly was had been hiding inside her the whole time. She'd cracked open like an eggshell and the girl she thought she was had disappeared. In her place was a bigger, better, badder version of herself. Someone who was capable.

"I guess now I'm in the society you don't need to teach me *the ways* anymore," Mason said, wiggling his fingers like a magician.

Sage passed him her helmet and smiled. "I guess not."

"Then why did you want me to bring you here?" he asked, and although he waited for her reply, his sly smirk told her that he knew the answer already.

Sage shrugged, her eyes landing on his barely parted lips. She watched him pout those lips and turn to flick out the kickstand. There was no denying what she wanted.

Mason hopped off his bike and faced the track that

lead to the lookout. Without looking at her he splayed his arm as if he were a butler. "Shall we?"

His brown hair fell in a wave and hovered above his defined jaw line. He was wearing a black hoodie, ripped jeans, and those blue shoes Sage hated. And she couldn't have liked this moron any more.

He took one step. That's all that Sage could bear. She rushed forward and wrapped her fingers around his wrist, gently tugging on his arm to turn him around. His eyes fell on her, a soft smile turning into a grin.

Sage let his wrist go, and moving her grip to his collar, she pulled him closer. Mason sucked in a breath as his green irises darted between her eyes and her mouth. She lifted her chin, reaching up on her tip toes to close the gap.

"Yes," he cheered as their lips connected.

It was better than before. Soft yet firm. Mason placed his hands on either side of her face, fingertips sliding through her hair. Her body warmed and she leaned in, pressing herself against him. His grip changed, holding her tighter with every second. He moved his hands down her body and grasping at her waist, he kissed her deeper, hungrier.

Sage felt the tips of his fangs, graze over her lips. She opened her eyes to find two ruby-like eyes staring back at her. He'd half-shifted. And looking at a circle of purple reflecting in his irises, she knew she had, too. As they pulled away, Sage noticed their auras melding together, a swirl of purple and red surrounding them.

Mason gave her a quick, soft kiss and sighed. "Oh Floss, you taste better than bourbon."

"Thank you," she replied, voice rich with sarcasm.

He smiled, stroking his thumb down one side of her face. "And man, I freaking adore you."

A sudden rush of embarrassment washed over her. Heat colored her cheeks and she glanced away. Almost immediately, Mason gently tugged on her chin, forcing her to make eye contact.

"I mean it. And what I said in my dorm, I meant it. I care about you."

Sage nodded. "I know, it's just... Everything is good. I'm not used to it. I have a new family, a great mentor..." she hesitated, but his eyes—open and welcoming—gave her comfort, a safety she hadn't known since her parents died. "And, I have you."

"Yes." Mason nodded fiercely. "You do."

They both returned to human form. Sage's wings took a little longer to retract than her talons. She took a breath, shaking off the tension.

"Speaking of family." She eased into the question. "How's Ben? Is he awake yet?"

Mason raised his brow. "He's okay. He woke up earlier this morning." He turned his gaze to the trees. "I'm hopeful. If I keep him close and train him well..." His voice petered out.

Sage grabbed his hand. She began walking to the track, pulling at him to follow. "Come on."

As they broke through the forest and took step onto the rock, Sage let his hand go and sat on a boulder. Above them, a cloud made way for sunshine. Sage smiled and untied her boots.

"What the heck are you doing, Floss?" Mason asked.

Sage slid her feet out of her boots and ripped her socks off. Placing her socks inside the boots, her smile widened. "Just something my mom told me to do."

"Okay." Mason plonked himself beside her and took his own shoes off.

Sage resisted the urge to throw them over the cliff. She pressed the soles of her feet onto cool stone and took a deep breath. Lifting her face to the sun, she said, "So, rookie, how does it feel to be in the society?"

"Rookie?" Mason raised his eyebrows. "All right, sure, I'll accept that. To answer your question? Yeah, it feels pretty damn good."

Sage leaned over, bumping her shoulder into his

side. "We're all here for you, I hope you know that."

"I know." Mason bumped her back, then frowned. "I'm sorry I wasn't there for you. That you had to face AJ alone."

A light breeze rustled through the trees and a rush of air licked at her bare feet. Sage wriggled her toes and stretched out her legs. She turned her head to Mason, resting her chin in front of her shoulder. "I think I needed it, you know? It taught me that I'm not just a distraction."

"Ha!" Mason shook his head. "You are so much more than a distraction."

Her heart bloomed. "It's weird, you know. I turned you, thinking I had broken the rules. The whole time, I felt like I was failing and that my world was about to crumble around me, but it all led to victory, and my world opened up."

Mason's eyes twinkled and a cocky smile lifted the edges of his mouth. "That's life isn't it? Just when you feel like giving up something magical is waiting around the next bend." He dusted his shoulder.

"Are you saying *you're* the something magical?" Sage teased.

Mason rolled his bottom lip out and shrugged.

Sage bit her lip, wondering if she should tell him the truth of what she meant.

"Oh my god, stop looking at me like that." Mason covered his face with his hand.

"Well, I'm not sure if you know that I was actually talking about me and what I've discovered in myself."

Mason laughed and tucked a stray hair behind her ear. "I know, Floss. I'm just teasing. Besides, I wouldn't call myself magical, I'm more mysterious or ethereal."

Sage thwacked his chest with the back of her hand. Before she'd even had the chance to make another move, Mason wrapped his arms around her, locking her arms at her sides. He pulled her into him, hugging her tight.

He whispered into her hair, "Thank you for following your instincts with me."

The recruits sat side-by-side across the front row. All of them were a little tired and a little confused, but not broken. And definitely stronger. A proper unified team. They were the Shadow Society as it was meant to be.

Makoto walked in. He took one step and stopped, staring at his students all together in a row. Smiling to himself, he locked the door.

He cleared his throat and headed for the back of the room. Pressing the button that opened the secret cage, he said, "I guess today's lesson is how to deal with a Fallen."

The wall behind his desk opened, revealing Arielle inside. She hardly blinked as her dark cage became a viewing room. She moved to the window and slammed her forehead against the glass, scowling at everyone.

"I think this is a better punishment than death," Camila joked.

As Makoto walked to his desk, he stated, "There'll be no more reciting at the end of class."

"Why?" Nadya asked, shocked. "One recruit turns someone, and we throw them out the window?"

Makoto took his place in front of his desk. He leaned against it, crossing his ankles. "Forget the rules, you're a clan now. It's taken a little longer than normal, but given you were infiltrated by a Fallen, I think you've done fairly well. From here on in, you all make the rules. As a family, you decide what to do. And I'll be here for support."

He placed his palms over the edge of his desk and half turned toward Arielle. "First point of order... you don't want me to kill Arielle? So, what do we do? How will you stop her from bringing more Fallen? Ruining lives? Killing innocents?"

Sage stared at Arielle through the glass. She'd moved away from the window and sat at the back of the cage, picking at her fingernails. An idea sparked in Sage's mind. She waited for Nadya or Caspar to speak. But everyone was silent.

"Well," Makoto said, crossing his arms. "We're off to a great start. If we can't think of anything, I'll have no other option—"

"What if," Sage spoke up. Everyone glanced her way—some surprised, some eager. "What if we forced her to go to the Veil? Can the Elders of the Veil take her? I mean, we can certainly contain a house cat, can't we?"

Makoto's brow dropped. His eyes drifted to the floor. The clan leaned forward on their chairs, awaiting their mentor's response. Lifting his head, he replied, "It's not a terrible idea. We can't technically banish her to the Veil, not like that. But if she's in the cage long enough, she's sure to get hungry or bored." His eyes slowly lit up. "And if she goes through to the Veil and leaves her cat, we take it somewhere else, somewhere she can't find it to reconnect into this world... Yes, it could work."

"What about the Veil?" Nadya asked. "Will that disrupt things? I'm guessing it wouldn't be great to have a bunch of Fallen wandering around."

Camila gave a loud huff. "One. There'd be one Fallen, not a whole army."

"Yeah, and Arielle won't be strong, she won't have claws or fangs," Caspar added.

"Right." Makoto clicked his fingers at Caspar. A second later, he pressed his palms against his temples. "I've never done anything like this before."

"I like it," Camila urged. "It's better than killing her. Although, if it fails I've got no problems with killing her."

"Camila!" Nadya moaned.

"What?" Camila said, giving Nadya a teasing smirk. "Just saying it as it is. And, I said *if* not *when*."

Makoto let his hands fall to his sides. He pushed himself away from his desk and paced in front of them. "Is this how we deal with her? I'm not opposed to it, but you're the clan, I'm just here to help you, however you decide."

Mason clapped his hands together and said, "Let's do it!"

Sage sat back in her chair. A bubble of excitement simmered in her gut. She knew there'd had to be another way.

"Great!" Makoto exclaimed. He took a moment to catch the eye each of the recruit separately, rubbing his hands with glee. "Now, onto the next point of business. The last part of the year, I want to ensure you'll be all right in the world alone. You know you won't have me forever. I'll have a new set of recruits to lead. So, let's choose an Alpha."

*Mason would make a great Alpha,* Sage thought, turning to look at him. He smiled back at her and slid his hand into hers. He jerked his chin up, motioning behind her.

She twisted around, finding Camila grinning at her. Camila took her other hand and squeezed. On the other side of Camila, Nadya and Caspar peered around, both sets of eyes shining with approval. Sage's heart fell to her stomach then began beating in double time. The whole clan, they were all looking at *her.*

"It's unanimous." Makoto said, beaming. "Do you accept the leadership, Sage?"

"W...Wait a minute," Sage said, slipping her hand from Camila's and reaching for her necklace.

As she smoothed her fingers along the leather, her mother's words rang loud and true. A new mantra echoed through her mind. *Believe in yourself.*

Sage called her owl forward, aligning into half-shift. She felt the purple aura envelop her. With Guardian strength running through her veins, she faced Makoto.

"I accept."

- - THE END - -

# ABOUT THE AUTHOR

Elle Scott lives in the Huon Valley, Tasmania, Australia with her husband, two sons, three cats, and one big ball of fluff, Labrador.

Telling stories has always been a part of her. When she was young, it was her dream to be a famous actress, and she would spend hours playing "make believe" with her sister. Her wild imagination turned everyday moments in life into extraordinary events. A long bus ride became an adventurous trek on the back of a horse galloping on the beach; or days spent in her backyard became days in the African Safari! Her imagination took her from her warm bed into a world where humans can shift into animals. Her biggest thrill is taking her oddball dreams and making them a reality with words.

Elle also tells real stories for real people. She is a multi-award winning family photographer.

Elle hopes to one day run workshops for self-conscious women, to turn them from a wallflower into a wildflower and give them the confidence to chase their dreams with ferocity.

## FOLLOW ELLE:
Instagram - @ellescott_author
Facebook - @ellescottauthor


## JOIN ELLE'S VIP LIST TODAY
And receive this short story for free

BETWEEN THE EARTH AND THE STARS follows
Arylia, who is an unwelcome alien seeking refuge on Earth.
Will her inexplicable friendship with Kyson, a law-abiding
soldier, doom the planet?

www.ellescottbooks.com/sign-up